THE GOOD 365 DAYS

WHERE LOVE MEETS DESTINY

EKNOOR JUNEJA

Made with ♥ on the Notion Press Platform
www.notionpress.com

I dedicate this book to my beloved father, Deepak Kumar Juneja.

I am eternally grateful to my father who inspired me to explore the field of reading and writing. His love and trust encouraged me in every single way and shall forever be.

I thank my family, especially my mother and my dear grandparents for showing their patience and gracious ways which helped me in writing this book without any hesitation.

Last but not least, I also thank my close friends, Deepshikha, Gayathry and Saksham for their unwavering support throughout and for believing in me all the way.

Contents

1. Chapter 1 1
2. Chapter 2 5
3. Chapter 3 8
4. Chapter 4 11
5. Chapter 5 17
6. Chapter 6 23
7. Chapter 7 29
8. Chapter 8 31
9. Chapter 9 52
10. Chapter 10 56
11. Chapter 11 58
12. Chapter 12 61
13. Chapter 13 66
14. Chapter 14 69
15. Chapter 15 75
16. Chapter 16 77
17. Chapter 17 81
18. Chapter 18 84
19. Chapter 19 89
20. Chapter 20 93
21. Chapter 21 94

CHAPTER ONE

Today is the most important day for Amaya. Amaya works as an employee in a magazine company in the US. She has been living in California for the past 2 years and is just 24 years old. Spring has just begun and today is the day when she has an annual fest exhibition of the magazines in her office like every year and also today, she is in charge of managing and everything very carefully as always. She is known to be the most eligible employee as per her Boss, Ms. Russell Smith, although she was young. It is just 7:00 AM. She had to reach her office by 8:00 AM. It's time for her to wake up but she's still sleeping.

The phone rang and it was 7:45 AM when she picked it up.

"Hello...?" Amaya answers in a sleepy tone.
"Where the hell are you Amaya?" Shouted Ms.Russell from the other side.
"Oh!" Amaya exclaimed, worried and checked what time it was.
"Yes, ma'am I'm on my way."
"I'm stuck in the traffic. Just coming," she added.
"Ok. Come fast. The Guests will arrive by 9," said her boss and cut the call.

Amaya ran fast towards the bathroom and got ready in 5 minutes. She packed her breakfast and had it on the way in her taxi. She managed to reach till 8:15 AM.

"Where were you? Everyone's waiting for you to help them decorate," Ms.Russell said in a worried tone.
"I'm so sorry ma'am," Amaya apologized.
"Okay. But there's hardly any time left for us to do the decorations so please just go and join them," said Ms. Russell.

"Okay..." Amaya was just going when the boss cut her.
"Oh, and yes Mr. Steward called and he was looking for some day when we could talk to him and place his order for our yet-to-launch magazine. So, whenever you're free just look at it," Ms. Russell added.
"Okay, sure ma'am. I'll look over it." Saying this Amaya rushed towards her cabin. She took out all the decorative materials that were needed and then called Sophie in her office. She handed over all the materials to her and told her whatever was to be done.
"The ribbons and the 'Welcome' heading are to be used for decorating the Lobby. Use the rest of the materials for the office and the party hall and also tell Ron to look over the ordering of the food and other stuff. Okay?" finished Amaya.
"Yes, I'll handle this stuff and will tell Ron about it. Don't worry," and then left Sophie.

After half an hour had passed Amaya went around to check over the decorations. The office had been decorated beautifully and she was highly impressed by the decorations done by the rest of her colleagues. Ms. Russell also appreciated their work and thanked Amaya for handling all this stuff so perfectly. By the next 15 minutes, the guests started coming to their annual fest exhibition. Almost all the magazines sold out successfully.

The guests were highly impressed by everybody's work and so they congratulated Ms. Russell and all her colleagues for their efforts and hard work reflected in such a short time. The day passed and all the employees including Ms. Russell decided to party that night for their achievement.

Amaya, Sophie, Ron, Nick, Mira, Jack, Ammie, Ms. Russell, everybody was present. The celebrations were done on Amaya's terrace.

Amaya and Jack served the drinks. On behalf of the victory, Ms. Russell raised a toast.

"For us!" she exclaimed, raising her glass in the air.
"For us!" everybody repeated.

"So, everybody did a great job today and I'm thankful to you all. And especially Amaya who brought us the respective materials that were needed. Thank You, Amaya," said Ms. Russell.

"You're welcome, ma'am, after all, it was my duty," Amaya said thankfully.

"Amaya, why don't you take up some time off for yourself? You can go on a holiday. Someplace where you can relax a bit," Ms. Russell suggested.

"You never get time for yourself honey and just keep doing this office work," she added.

"No, no ma'am please I don't need to do all this right now. Also, there are so many projects pending. So, how am I supposed to go on a holiday?" Amaya said.

"Oh, come on honey..." Ms. Russell was speaking when Amaya cut her and said in a soft tone, "Ma'am, maybe some other time?"

"Okay. As you wish. But whenever you require a holiday just tell me. And no need to hesitate," Ms. Russell completed.

"Sure ma'am," Amaya smiled.

After that only Nick stood up in excitement.

"So, guys, maybe this party will get boring if we do not do something exciting. So, does anybody know of any game?" Mira jumped up in excitement.

"I know. I know a game," she said.

"So, madam, please do the honour of telling us about the game," Nick said and sat down.

"Okay, now listen. The game's name is Consequences. Each player takes a sheet of paper and folds it into four. First, draw a head (animal, human or imaginary), fold the paper down to hide the drawing- but leave some neck- and pass it on. Next, draw a torso, arms or wings, fold the paper (leaving the tops of the legs showing) and pass on..." She was speaking but was cut in between by Sophie.

"Oh, that means we'll draw a monster?"

"Oh no, Dumbo! Ssh and just listen to me," Mira said, giving a rude reaction. "Um where was I? Ok then come the legs (fold again). Pass on. Finally, add the feet. Unfold. You'll be amazed," she added and gave a clap.

Everyone was excited and agreed to play the game. Amaya ran towards her bedroom and brought 8 pages and some pens and distributed them. Everybody started their drawings. After 20 minutes everybody was ready to open their pages and see what blunder they had done.

"Ready one, two. And three open," Mira said.

After two seconds all of them were laughing uncontrollably. Everyone had made something like the head floating in the air, the legs dancing, the body of a fish and so on...

It was 12:45 AM when everyone decided to get back home.

"Bye Amaya. Night-Night," everybody said and left.
"Bye, guys. Night-Night," Amaya smiled and then shut the door.

Amaya picked up her car keys from the bed and threw them at the desk.

She quickly changed and then went off to bed.

CHAPTER TWO

Early in the morning at 8, Amaya woke up. She opened the curtains of her room and went into the balcony with her sleepy eyes. She picked up the sprinkler and started watering the plants. Her neighbours, Mr. and Mrs. Petersburg were walking down the lane. They waved at Amaya.

"A very good morning, Amaya," they said.
"Good morning, love birds," Amaya said, smiling at them.

Amaya kept the sprinkler back and walked towards the door to pick up the newspaper. When she picked up the newspaper, her phone rang.

"Hello?" her mom spoke.
"Hello. Good morning ma," Amaya said.
"How are you doing Amaya?" her mom asked.
"Am good. You tell me how you and Dad are there?" Amaya asked.
"We're fit and fine as always," her mom said and handed the phone over to her father.
"Hello, Amaya? How are you beta?" Her dad asked.
"I'm fine Dad. What are you doing?" Amaya asked.
"Oh, we are having a cup of our evening tea with biscuits," he said.
"You should visit India when free. We miss you," he added.
"I miss you too Dad but right now there is lots of work pending here. So many projects and you know," Amaya said.
"Ok then. But do come." He spoke.
"Of course, Dad I'll pay a visit soon. Bye," she said.
"Bye. God Bless," he said.

She went inside the kitchen and prepared some coffee for herself.

Taking the coffee outside, she started reading the newspaper. She flipped the pages on and on. On one of the pages, she saw an advertisement showing a lottery ticket. There was a quiz that would be taken online and whoever won would get a chance to win a free trip to Europe for 3 months.

She kept the coffee aside and started looking for some more information. She saw that there was a number given for getting more information. She quickly penned up the number and took out the ticket. On the back of the ticket was written the website where the participants had to appear. On the last page of the newspaper, there was a form given which was to be filled by the participants and had to be sent through post at their office in Los Angeles.

She quickly filled the form in excitement and got ready. She picked up her car keys and headed towards the post office which was 6 streets away from her home. Before she handed the post, she took out a stamp and put it on the card. After that, she headed towards Nicole's home. Nicole was more likely her elder brother. He opened the door and with a smile, Amaya hugged him.

"Hey!" she said.
"Hello, miss!" he said happily.

They both went in and sat down in Nicole's living area.

"So, how are you doing Nicole?" she asked.
"All good. And guess what!" he exclaimed.
"What?" she asked.
"I'm getting married!" he said excitedly.
"Oh. Oh My God!" Amaya said.
"Come here, boy," she stood up and hugged him.
"When did this happen? I mean who's that lucky girl hum?" she asked.
"4 days back only. I proposed to her," he said.
"Really? Well, that's so nice," she said.
"Yeah," he blushed.

"Um, coffee?" he asked.
"Yeah sure," she said.

Nicole brought the coffee for Amaya and himself.

"So, when is it?" Amaya asked.
"What?" He asked, looking confused.
"You wedding bro. When is it taking place? She asked.
"Oh, that. Yeah, that is taking place after 4 months," he said.
"Okay. So ready to give a fresh start to your life hmm," she said.
"Yeah. I'm 100% ready," he said confidently.
"Well, that's good, big boy," she said, poking him on his shoulder.
"Well. It was good seeing you. Now I have to leave," she added.
"Wait for some time," he requested.
"Oh no no no,, the thing is that I have to be at home and complete my office work. So, see you super soon. Okay," she said, hugging him.
"Okay then bye," he waved.
"Bye," she waved back.

After reaching home she ordered some pizza for herself. It was 7 in the evening when she sat down and started watching TV while eating some Pizza. It was her favourite movie that was being aired on TV, "*The Fault in Our Stars* "

She was so sleepy that day, she went to bed early. She dropped down on her bed and slept at 9:30 PM. She had a very tiring day, but a good one.

CHAPTER THREE

Amaya woke up at 6 in the morning and went jogging today. She thought of maybe covering her area in like 1 hour. While jogging she noticed a pamphlet for the same ad which she saw in the newspaper a day before. There was a number written on that. It said that it was of the guide that would guide the winner in Europe. His name was Michael. She noted the number given on her phone and went back home jogging. At her gate, she took out her water bottle from her side bag and drank some water. She prepared herself some breakfast and ate it while reading the newspaper. That's when her doorbell rang. It was Ammie with a water bottle in her hand.

"Hi! Good morning, Amaya," Ammie said and entered the house.
"Hey! Good morning, Ammie. So early today what happened? Is everything Ok?" Amaya asked.
"Yes-Yes everything's alright. I just came to the park nearby so I thought maybe I should meet you," Ammie said.
"Oh, for that Yoga class?" Amaya asked.
"Yup," Ammie said.
"Get seated. Let me bring some coffee for you," Amaya said and went to the kitchen.

Ammie sat on the sofa and just then she noticed that the phone number was saved as "Michael the Guide."

"Hey, what's this?" she asked.
"Oh, that? Nothing," Amaya said.
"Amaya, at least you can tell me," Ammie said.
"Okay." Amaya after a long breath said, "I was just planning to, you know,

maybe I should take a leave like Ms. Russell just told me," She said hesitantly.
"Okay, so what did you plan?" Ammie asked.
"I did not plan exactly but first I have to win," Amaya said.
"Win? What win?" Ammie asked, confused.
"Umm, I filled a form for a lottery kind of thing which said the participants are going to appear on an online quiz. The topic will be given soon and whoever is the winner is going to get a free trip to Europe for 3 months," Amaya said.
"Oh God. 3 months. Free?" she shockingly asked.
"Yup. It's 3 months and that too, free," Amaya said.
"So, when is this quiz going to take place?" Ammie asked.
"After 1 week exact," Amaya answered.
"Okay. So, all the best babe," Ammie said.
"Thanks. And oh, I need to tell you some great news," Amaya said excitedly.
"What?" Ammie asked.
"Nicole's getting married!" she shouted in excitement.
"What? Oh my God. When did this happen? I mean how?" Ammie asked, jumping off the sofa happily.
"Only a few days back. He just proposed to his sister's best friend and the wedding is going to take place in 4 months," Amaya said happily.
"And soon he is going to have a get-together," she added.
"Okay so finally he got his girl," Ammie said.
"Okay, now I got to go. Mom must be waiting for me," she added and left.
"Okay," Amaya said.

She, in the next 30 minutes, got ready to go to the office. Today she took her car and drove straight away towards her office.

She reached there by 8. She parked her car in the basement and took the lift.

"Which floor madam?" the lift handler asked.
"7th floor it is," Amaya said.
"Okay, madam," he said.

The moment she stepped out of the lift she met Ron.

"Hey! Morning," she said energetically.
"Good morning Amay!" he said.
"You look great and full of energy today. What happened?" he asked.
"Nothing. Just jogged after so long. It's just so beautiful to get some fresh and cool air", she said.

After that only they both went to their respective places together.

Amaya had tons of work today. First, she had to call Mr. Steward and fix a meeting. She got a call from Ms. Russell stating her work that was to be done. She sent some files to Amaya that were to be completed in the next 3 hours. She started filling up the files. Ms. Russell made her responsible for designing some new covers for their upcoming magazines and they had to be kind of ethnic. Those designs were to be submitted after 2 days.

Amaya had overtime and a very hectic day. She reached home at 10:00 PM that night. She quickly ate her dinner and slept by 11:00 PM.

CHAPTER FOUR

Today Amaya woke up by 6:30 in the morning and went for a jog. She covered the area in about 45 minutes. She went back home by 7:30 AM. When she reached home, she had her breakfast and went to her bedroom. She was really confused about what she should wear that day.

"What should I wear today? Oh God!"

She was confused. She took out 2 dresses from her closet.

"This one or that one? I am in no mood to go to the office today. But it is important just because of that meeting. Ugh!!" she said in anger.

She finally chose her dress. She decided to wear a dark blue coloured middy.

She got ready in the next 20 minutes. She did her make-up well. She looked magnificent today. Her beauty was beyond anyone's reach.

She reached the office by 8:20 AM. When she was going towards the lift someone from behind came up.

"Lovely!" It was a very handsome guy, looking neat, someone who was not known to her.
"Pardon. Do I know you?" Amaya asked.
"Of course not. Let me introduce myself to you. I am Samuel James and I am new to this place. I just got transferred from North Dakota to California. I am best known for creating magazine covers. So, this is me," he said.
"Okay. My name is Amaya and I have been working over here for the last 2

years and my boss never gets mad at me," she giggled.
"What's your age by the way?" Samuel asked.
"I am 24. And you?" Amaya asked.
"I am 25 and will be turning 26 this year," he spoke.
"Oh, well, that's good," she said while getting out of the lift.

Ms. Russell saw both of them.

"Welcome home baby!" Ms. Russell spoke to Samuel.
"Hey!" Samuel gave her a tight hug.
"Baby?" Amaya asked in confusion.
"Oh, yes, Amaya meet my son Samuel. From today he is going to work with us," she said happily.
"Ok, so now I understand the 'Sam' you always talked about is actually Samuel," Amaya turned towards him.
"I'm sorry I didn't recognize you," she added.
"That's ok. There's no problem with that. By the way you look..." After a long pause he said, "Um, you look very beautiful," Samuel told Amaya.
"Thanks," Amaya gave him a polite smile.
"Sweetie, Mr. Steward is going to come any minute. So, please be ready. It's already late," Ms. Russell hurried to the conference hall.
"But it's only 8:30 AM now," she said, confused.
"Yes, I know that it's 8:30 AM. Mr. Steward just changed his time from 9:30AM to 9AM this morning," she held some files.
"Ok then, I must go now," Amaya said.

Amaya entered her cabin and kept her bag on the table.

"Oh shit. I mean what on earth is happening? Am I not allowed to just relax for a little while?" Amaya got irritated.
"Whoa-Whoa, why are you mad?" Samuel entered and asked.
"What are you doing here?" Amaya questioned him.
"Oh! Me?" Samuel asked.
"Yes. You," Amaya said.
"Because I am just not able to take my eyes off you," Samuel murmured.

"What did you just say?" Amaya stared at him.

"Oh. Nothing. I just, um, I just came to see you," Samuel said, giving a weird smile.

"And why would you do that? We hardly know each other. Isn't it?" Amaya said.

"So what? We can get to know each other. I am Samuel, son of your sweet boss. I am 25. I am going to turn 26 this year," Samuel was stopped by Amaya in between his introduction.

"Wait! Maybe some other time?" she politely asked.

"Maybe during lunch in the cafeteria," she added.

"Okay? But where is it?" he asked.

"Near the entrance," she said.

"Okay," he said.

"Now, if you may excuse me for a while, till the meeting gets over because it's already time," she spoke.

"Okay then. I'll meet you in the cafeteria," he said and left.

"Hmm," she said.

The meeting was over by 10:45 AM, after which Amaya rushed towards the cafeteria. Samuel was sitting in the corner near the window side.

"Oh. Hi!" Samuel got up and greeted her.

"Hey!" Amaya in a low tone.

"Hectic schedule?" Samuel asked.

"Yes. I am feeling as if I am going to doze off and sleep right now," Amaya said.

"Wait. Let me order something for you. You look really tired," Samuel called for a waiter.

"Two cappuccinos along with two chocolate brownies," he ordered.

"Well. That's my favourite!"

"Mine too," Samuel smiled.

Both of them giggled.

"So, now can you permit me to introduce myself to you?"

"No," Amaya said.

"But why?" he asked.

"Because you forgot that you already did," She peeped on her phone.

"When did I do that?"

"In the lift."

"Oh, that was nothing though. I have a brilliant idea," he took the order.

"Tell me about it," Amaya was excited.

"You can ask me about whatever you wish to know about me and I'll answer you honestly," Samuel suggested.

"Okay then. So, my first question to you is, from where did you graduate?"

"Cambridge University, United Kingdom. Then I got a job in North Dakota and now I am here," he sipped his cappuccino.

"Okay, my next question to you is why did you choose this job? I mean to say why do you love photography so much?" Amaya smiled.

"Photography is my universe in itself. The feeling of capturing moments is just great. It is mesmerizing and beautiful to capture the precious moments of life. Photography isn't just a passion, it's an art," he spoke candidly.

"So that totally shows your love for photography is endless," Amaya said.

"You can say so," Samuel said.

"Did you have any girlfriends in the past?" Amaya was eager to know.

"Naah," Samuel answered very casually.

"So, why are you still single hmm?"

"I am not interested right now. I suppose I am still finding a girl that loves me and not that treats me as a total joke," he laughed.

"What kind of girl are you looking for?" she inquired.

"I am. Wait. Why are you asking that to me? I mean, are you in the mood of opening a marriage bureau or what?" Samuel questioned her.

"Oh no. Of course not. I am just casually asking these questions," Amaya sipped the cappuccino.

"Okay!" he ate the brownie.

"So, my next question to you is," Amaya was speaking while her phone rang.

"Hello?" Amaya spoke.

"Hello Amy!" the voice spoke.

"Sorry, but who is it?" She was confused.

"Oh man, it's me, Daisy," The voice said.

Daisy Anthony. Amaya's best friend. In fact, she was more like a sister to her. It had been a long time since they met. They had been together since they were in grade 9. They were always together when they lived in India.

"Oh! Hey Dora," Amaya happily said.
"How are you? Long time, no see," she added.
"I'm all fine. You tell me about yourself. How are you doing? How's your job?" Daisy asked.
"Everything is fine over here and I am doing great. I really miss you. Where are you, bro?" Amaya asked.
"Actually, I am at your place right now," Daisy happily answered.
"What? At my place! I am coming there right now. Just wait. I'll be there in 15 minutes, Okay!" Daisy jumped in excitement.

Both the girls were excited to see each other after so long. It's been 4 years since they had seen each other.

"Who was it?" Samuel asked.
"Daisy," Amaya picked up her bag.
"Will you come with me?" she asked.
"Okay. But who is she?"
"I am going to tell you everything but right now I am in a hurry," Amaya stood and ran towards the basement.

They both reached her home in exactly 15 minutes but Amaya could not find Daisy anywhere; she got worried about getting pranked by her. But then only- "Boom!" Daisy came from behind making Amaya laugh.

"Hey Bro! What's up?" Daisy gave her a tight hug.
"Hey! I missed you," Amaya smiled.
"I missed you too. You know, the thing is that I came here to tell you that I am getting transferred over here and I am looking for a place to live. So, maybe you can help me out with that," Daisy told her.
"Really! When is that going to happen? I am waiting for that day. We are

not separating again. I am surely going to help you but you have to promise me that you will stay with me. Until you finally find your new place,"

"Of course. Because I have many things to talk about," and then only she noticed Samuel.

"But who is this cute guy along with you? You never mentioned him before. Oh! Is he your boyfriend? Are you guys dating each other?" Daisy tried pulling her leg.

"No!" they both exclaimed together.

"No. Not at all. He is my new friend whom I met just today in the office and also, he is my boss's son. So, do not create any misunderstandings in your mind. Okay!" Amaya said, taking a deep breath.

"Okay! Don't worry babe. You know, I just thought. But then too, I apologize. Now are we going to stand up here the whole day or are we also going to get inside?" Daisy pulled her suitcases.

That day they all partied together and talked about many things. Even Samuel stayed with them. It was too late to go back home, so he was asked to stay there only.

The day went extremely well for all of them.

They all were exhausted. Daisy went to her room and dozed off. She had many more things to discuss with Amaya.

CHAPTER FIVE

Since it was an off day today, everybody woke up late. It was 10 in the morning when they woke up. Nobody realized what was happening. In the morning Daisy woke up first. The moment she entered Amaya's room, what she saw confused her even more. Samuel and Amaya were sleeping, hugging each other tightly and were sleeping like they were very tired, not realizing when they had slept. Daisy took a picture of them and woke them up.

"Good morning, guys!" Daisy said loudly.

They both woke up.

"I suppose you both slept tight. Right?" Daisy told them.
"Yeah," Samuel said in a sleepy tone.
"I suppose you both want to see this," Daisy said.
"What is it?" Amaya asked.
"Ta-da!" The moment Daisy showed them their picture they went speechless.
"When did you hug me? I thought I hugged my Coco!" Amaya said.
"Coco? Who's that?" Samuel asked.
"My baby! Where are you?" Amaya went around to look for Coco.
"You never mentioned that you had a baby too," Samuel said.
"It's her teddy stupid," Daisy whispered to him.
"Teddy? Like seriously?" Samuel broke into laughter.
"I mean, you were looking for a teddy. Bahahaha...," Samuel couldn't control his laughter.
"What! Just wait for a second, I'll teach you how to laugh," Amaya said and threw a pillow at him.
"Aye stop!" Samuel started throwing the cushions on the other hand.

They both were fighting like kids.

"Come on guys. Stop behaving like rats. Stop it," Daisy told them. Amaya went to the kitchen. Daisy followed her.
"Our first fight," Amaya thought.
"Ya," Daisy spoke.
"What?" Amaya asked.
"I said. Yes. This was your first fight. And that too for such a silly thing," Daisy said, biting an apple.
"How come you know what I am thinking?" Amaya asked.
"You know, I know you very well. Babe!" Daisy said.
"I am going to water the plants. Ok, babe?" Amaya said and went outside.
"Ok," Daisy left, taking another bite.

The moment she entered the lawn Samuel scared her.

"Now what?" Amaya asked.
"Nothing," Samuel said.

Amaya took the pipe and started watering the plants. She looked beautiful.

"Such a beauty," Samuel stared at her.

Then only Daisy entered and noticed Samuel. She perfectly knew that something was definitely going on inside his head.

"Hey!" Daisy jumped beside him.
"Hey! Has she had a boyfriend? Ever?" Samuel asked Daisy.
"OMG! He is asking this for her. I truly want to set them up, man," Daisy thought.
"Hey? Where are you lost?" Samuel asked.
"Oh. No. She never had a boyfriend. Neither has she fallen in love. She is still in search of a good boy," Daisy told him.
"Good boy? As in?" Samuel asked.

"Good boy as in terms of being honest, understanding and especially someone who loves her," Daisy said.
"Do you think if I fall for her then she is going to accept me?" Samuel asked her.
"Maybe. I mean, I don't know. You can try at least," Daisy said.
"But how?" Samuel said.
"How do I know? And by the way, it's been just one day since you guys have known each other," Daisy said.
"Ya. But you know I have never felt like this for someone before. Like ever," Samuel said.

And at last, he said.

"I think I have fallen for her," and that was what shocked Daisy.
"Here's your chance then," Daisy said smiling.

Samuel went ahead. Daisy went inside and turned on the music.

"Chand Sifarish" of Fanaa. Samuel also loved Hindi songs as he was half Indian and half American.

He again scared her and then only her pipe went in the air and got stuck on the pole. It rained on their lawn. It was a romantic moment. Daisy saw them from the window.

"Aw! So cute," Daisy was standing in Amaya's bedroom watching them through the glass door.

She enjoyed the scenery. They both danced together. Suddenly, it started raining for real. They both enjoyed it. That day went great for them.

"Breakfast time!" Daisy exclaimed as they entered.

Daisy gave them the towels.

"Here. Now freshen up fast, the food is waiting," Daisy told them. It was already 12:00. The sun was on their head.
"Come on guys," Daisy said.
"What?" Amaya asked while taking a bite of the salad.
"I just forgot to tell you that we have to go to a party," Daisy said.
"What party?" Amaya asked.
"My uncle and aunt live here. My sister is getting married. It's her mehndi today. We have to dress traditionally," Daisy said.
"Okay. I'm going to get ready then," Amaya said.

Samuel was also excited to go and went inside to get ready.

"Samuel. Where are you going to get the clothes from?" Daisy asked.
"Here, take them. Amaya handed over a dress to him. It was a kurta-pyjama.
"Whose are these?" Samuel asked.
"My father's dress. The one that was worn by him at a wedding 2 years back. I only have this right now so I thought that maybe it will work for now," Amaya said.
"Ok. Thanks," Samuel said.

Everybody got ready instead of Amaya. Samuel was looking just like a gentleman.

"Whoa, look at you. You look smart," Daisy said.

And then only, Amaya stepped out of her room.

"Oh-My-God! A fairy just stepped out," Daisy said, looking at Amaya.

The moment Samuel took a look at her, he had no words to express her beauty.

"Alluring!" Samuel said.

Amaya was wearing a beautiful saree. The one which was worn by her mother on the day of her engagement. It was a beautiful light blue saree with beautiful patterns on it.

"Thanks," Amaya said.
"Now let's go," Daisy said. But Samuel stood still with his mouth open.
"Samuel. Let's go," Daisy added.
"Ha? Yes. Let's go," Samuel was astonished.
"She is looking so very beautiful. Oh, she's such an angel," Samuel was lost in his own thoughts.

They had to leave early because the function was in the neighbouring town. Daisy drove and Amaya sat next to her. Samuel was not able to take his eyes off her. Daisy caught him.

"Stop Staring," Daisy said.
"What are you talking about?" Amaya asked.
"Nothing. That guy on the street was just staring at me. Right, Samuel?" Daisy said.
"Yeah. Right," Samuel watched out of the window.

They reached the place at around 6:00 in the evening. They entered the hall and saw the guests chatting. The women were settled in the Mehndi area.

"Go get some mehndi on," Samuel suggested.

All the guys out there took Samuel on the stage and everybody started to dance. They gave a shout-out to the ladies for a dance. Amaya was getting her mehndi done. After 15 minutes or so Amaya was done with her mehndi. All the eyes caught her. She looked as if she was the bride.

"OMG! Stunning babe!" Daisy came to her.
"Like seriously? What's so special in wearing this mehndi?" Amaya said.
"No really. Look, you just got everybody's attention. All the guys have their eyes stuck on you," Daisy said giggling.

They both laughed.

It was the time to dance for all the couples, after about half an hour.

Samuel came to Amaya and asked her for a dance. "May I?" He bowed a little in the hope of getting her hand.

First Amaya looked at Daisy. It was a "Go-Go" from her side. Daisy was excited to watch them both dance together.

"Um- Okay," Amaya said.

Samuel held her hand and took her to the stage. Samuel and Amaya danced together. After the party was over, they all were extremely tired. This time Samuel drove back towards Amaya's home. They reached home at quarter to 2 at night and soon dozed off to sleep.

CHAPTER SIX

It was roughly 6 hours after which Amaya's phone rang.

"Hello?" Amaya said in a very sleepy tone, her eyes shut, with her face on the pillow.
"Hello Amaya," the voice said.
"Who's this?" Amaya said, yawning.
"Amaya, this is me, Ms. Russell. What happened? Are you okay? I can call maybe later then," Ms. Russell spoke.
"Oh. Good morning, ma'am. I am so sorry; I didn't recognize you. I just woke up," Amaya said.
"Amaya, I just called to have a word with Sam. He is just not picking up the phone, so I got worried if he's fine," Ms. Russell told her.
"Yes, sure ma'am. He is sleeping. And snoring! So, maybe he did not get to hear the ring. I'll just hand over the phone to him," Amaya went near Samuel. She kept her hand on the phone. She started poking him.

"Sam?"
"Sam,"
"Sam!"

She screamed in a low tone.

"Huh, Hun. What? Who's there? I'll shoot you," he spoke. Amaya's expression had to be seen.
"Hey. It's me. Why on earth are you acting so weird? I mean are you a cowboy or something in your dreams? Anyways, here's the phone," Amaya said, making him catch the phone.
"What for?" he asked.

"It's your mum dude," she said, jumping on the bed and dozing off to sleep again.
"Hello?" he said.
"Sam! Are you even behaving over there? Because I don't think so," Ms. Russell said.
"I think so too," Amaya said, pointing up in the air with her eyes closed.
"What. Sam? This was not expected," Ms. Russell said.
"Mom! Chill. Just Relax. I am not that way," Samuel said.
"Oh really?" Ms. Russell and Amaya both spoke together. Just by chance.
"Ma, please. Okay tell me what was the reason for you calling me" he asked.
"Yes. I wanted to tell you that we are organizing a trip," she said.
"Trip? Where?" Samuel asked.

After hearing this Amaya bounced up the bed and started listening carefully. The phone was now kept on speaker mode.

"To Europe. It's a three-month trip. There was a lottery that came in the newspaper a few days back. The trip sponsor is providing us with a free package because of our deal with them. It's a ticket for 3. So maybe you, Amaya and somebody else can go," She spoke.
"And why not you?" Samuel questioned her.
"I am sorry but I can't go because I have to go to Chicago for a meeting, baby," Ms. Russell said.
"So, you'll not come at all. I mean if there's a chance of you joining us maybe?" Samuel asked.
"Nope," she said.
"I can go," Daisy said standing at the entrance.
"Well. Who's that?" Ms. Russell asked.
"Oh, that's a friend of Amaya," Samuel said.
"Okay. Then that's great. The ticket for three will not get cancelled. I'll just send the tickets there. Maybe till noon," Ms. Russell said.
"Okay bye," Samuel said.

Daisy and Amaya jumped on the bed in excitement.

"Amay!!!!"
"Daisy!"

Both of them shouted in excitement.

"You know what. This was the trip that I was planning for a few days back. But I did not know that this dream would come true and that too for free. Oh my God," Amaya was so happy saying this.
"Really? Then you should always make a habit of dreaming about something, Amy," Daisy said, still very excited.

Amaya was so very happy that she went and hugged Samuel.

They all jumped in excitement. They then went out for breakfast. At 12:15 they received the itinerary regarding the trip. Amaya called both of them in the dining room. They sat on the sofa while Amaya read the itinerary loud and clear.

"The information is as follows:" Amaya started reading.

"3 Month Backpacking Trip Itinerary

- *London- United Kingdom- 4-5 Days*
- *Paris- France- 4-5 Days*
- *Nice- France- 2-3 Days*
- *Florence- Italy- 2-3 Days*
- *Rome- Italy- 6-7 Days +++*
- *Interlaken- Switzerland- 2-3 Days*
- *Zurich- Switzerland- 3-4 Days*
- *Munich- Germany- 3-4 Days*
- *Vienna- Austria- 3-4 Days +*
- *Bratislava- 3-5 Days*
- *Prague- 3-4 Days*
- *Berlin- 4 Days*
- *Copenhagen- Denmark- 3 Days- With a side trip to Tivoli*

- *Brussels and Bruges- Belgium- 4 Days*
- *Amsterdam- 4 Days Max,"* Amaya finished.

And then Samuel spoke, "62 days in cities calculated using max days we have and 1 day of travel between each 79 days 11 days left to make plans for a total of 90 days,"

**All these are within a decent circuit of each other and we'll be flying for parts.*

"Wow. Mathematics master you are. Huh. But how did you do that? And there's no need for our opinions because this is enough for the trip. But if you need our opinions, then we can say that the only thing that needs to be done is shopping," Amaya asked.
"Oh, that's nothing. We can do that in no time. So when are we supposed to leave?" Samuel asked.

Amaya quickly took a look at the itinerary again.

"The 12th of the succeeding month," Amaya announced.
"And today is?" Daisy went to look at the calendar.
"Oh my, today is the 30th. There's so much to do," Daisy added.
"Seriously, I mean there's hardly any time left. Any ideas of the places that I have missed?" She went through the itinerary again. "God! We have to go shopping first and then apply for the tickets," Amaya said.
"And so on. If you are going to give all the details about what is to be done then probably, we won't be able to do anything. So, move on then," Daisy said.
"Yes!" Samuel said.

They all got ready by the next hour. The girls were excited to go shopping.

Amaya and Daisy headed towards the mall whereas Samuel went on to apply for the visa.

Amaya and Daisy reached the mall and started looking for some cool handbags. The moment they entered they had a look at the Persian collection of baggage and then some Caprese ones.

"Oh man, I'm so excited for this trip. And that too a three-month trip. This is going to be so cool and relaxing," Daisy said.
"Really. I mean our life has just become like a 'boring drama'. Nowadays we hardly have any time for ourselves. I have been working for the last 2 years and I hardly take any leave, or, you can say that I hardly get any time to relax and chill out," Amaya said, giving the baggage at the counter.
"This is so damn true. Same thing with me," Daisy said.

Then they went shopping for some clothes. Amaya got one dress but it was too expensive. It cost $150 but it was so pretty that she decided to try it for once. It was a magenta one-piece, an off-shoulder. It fit her perfectly. But she did not tell Daisy about that dress. She wanted to surprise her by wearing that dress someday during the trip. That dress looked as if it was made for her.

They then headed for some footwear and then back home. They reached by 9:30 at night and Samuel had already reached home 2 hours ago.

That day, the dinner was prepared by him.

"Come on now, come for dinner," Samuel said.

Everybody sat for dinner. Samuel served dinner. That day's menu was homemade grilled chicken and pasta. Amaya decided to have only pasta and eggs as she was an eggetarian.

"Yum, tasty. From where did you get that?" Amaya asked.
"No, seriously. And from where is this tasty chicken ordered?" Daisy questioned too.
"I made it," Samuel said, giving a big smile.
"Really? I think you are a multi-talented man. You are a master in mathematics and now in cooking too. You are a genius," Amaya said.

"A loud round of applause for Mr. Genius," Daisy said. Both of them clapped for him.

"Thank you, ladies," Samuel said.

That was 'The Best Day' indeed.

CHAPTER SEVEN

"Good morning, Amaya!" Amaya woke up early in the morning, yawning and taking a stretch. She saw Samuel quietly sleeping. For the first time, she saw him like that. He was looking as if a baby was sleeping on his bed, looking ahead for big dreams.

Daisy came to Amaya sleepily rubbing her eyes.

"Happy morning Amy!" Daisy gave her a lazy hug.
"Good morning, Dora!" Amaya said.

Amaya got up from her bed and started looking for her phone. It was kept on the side table beside Samuel. The moment she was going to take the phone Samuel took a turn and his hand dropped on Amaya's hand and caught her. He was still sleeping. She gently tried to pull away from his hand but she couldn't.

She then gave it a last try and was successful in putting aside his hand and pulling out hers.

Daisy played romantic songs that woke up Samuel. Daisy started dancing. Amaya was still beside Samuel. The moment he saw Amaya turning he held her hand. She stared at him as if he would hold her hand again and again.

"Early morning music huh?" Samuel said.
Taking her hand away Amaya said, "Not me. It's Daisy who played that,"
"I already know that. A romantic morning it is. Wow," Samuel gave a pleasant smile to Amaya.
Opening the curtains Amaya said, "Exactly," Then there was another one.

"God Daisy! What is all this craziness for?" Amaya asked.
"I am very happy. And it's such a beautiful morning. Right, Sam?" Daisy handed him an apple.
"Yeah, I suppose," Samuel said.

Amaya waved her head but Daisy forced Amaya to dance with her.

Samuel enjoyed watching their dance. Their 'crazy dance'. But still, Amaya looked the best for him. His eyes were laid on Amaya's face, continuously watching her.

He loved her and he did not know whether Amaya was going to accept him as he is.

After a minute or so Samuel also joined them. He went crazy, dancing with them. Amaya and Samuel laid their eyes looking at each other.

He dreamt as if he danced with her and then pulled her towards him for real, and started dancing with her.

"Hey! Lost people," Daisy clicked her fingers.

They both felt awkward. A few days passed and they had been busy all the time, packing the luggage to be taken and poring over the rest of the things to be taken care of.

CHAPTER EIGHT

DAY-1 *(London – United Kingdom)*

"Come on Amy! How much more time? We are going to miss the flight," Daisy called out.

"One second Dora. Just checking if everything is kept," Amaya said. The phone rang.

"Hello?" Daisy said.

"Hey, Dora! All set?" It was Amaya's father.

Daisy then answered excitedly,

"Yup. By the way, how are you uncle?"

"I'm good. Okay, now there is no time left for discussions. You should probably leave now," he said.

"Yes. Your one and only daughter are wasting time," Daisy said.

"Okay. Tell her to relax and leave. Take care bye," her father said.

"For sure. Bye," Daisy said.

"Amy! What the hell are you doing in there? Come on. Just Relax and let's go," Daisy shouted.

Samuel came in, "What are you guys doing? I have been waiting for the past 25 minutes out there. Come fast now.

"Yeah, just coming," Daisy said, calling out for Amaya.

"Wait what? Amaya is not ready yet?" Samuel asked.

"Nope. She is still checking out for all the things," Daisy said.

"Yeah, I am here," Amaya came out running with her suitcase and baggage.

"Okay now, let's go. Come on!" Samuel said.

Meanwhile, when Amaya was locking the door, Samuel kept her suitcase in the taxi.

"Take care, Amaya. Have a safe and healthy journey child," Ms. Russell had come to see off.
"Thank you, ma'am," Amaya smiled and hugged her.

Daisy jumped off on the first seat. In the back seat, Amaya sat with Samuel.

"Bye Mom," Samuel said.
"Bye Sam. Call me once you reach," Ms. Russell said.
"Okay," Samuel waved goodbye.

They reached the airport in time. Their flight was to board by noon.

"Excuse me, Where would be the check-in counter for American Airlines?" Samuel asked one of the workers at the airport.
"Straight and then right, check-in counter No. 2," the worker told them.
"Thank you," Samuel said.

They all walked in towards counter no. 2 where the baggage was to be submitted.

"What time will your flight board sir?" The person sitting at the desk asked.
"Noon," Samuel said.
"On time sir. Your luggage is all ok sir. Have a nice flight sir," he spoke.
"Thank you," Samuel said.
"I took out all the eatables and water bottles from your bag," Daisy whispered to Amaya.
"What? I mean how could you do that Daisy? Now we don't have anything to eat and drink!" Amaya got worried.
"At least the food will not get wasted. Otherwise, if I had not taken all those eatables out, then due to being overweight they would have thrown them," Daisy told her. "We can buy something here which can be carried easily," she added.

"Okay now let's go," Amaya said.

They all sat in the aeroplane by 11:40 AM.

"I am going to sleep all the time during the flight," Daisy told Amaya.
Samuel then said, "Like seriously? I thought that we would just,"
"Just?" Daisy said.
"Well, I do not have any role in that. She is there to work with it," Daisy said.
"What? Is there some really important role to be played? By me," Amaya sarcastically asked.

Their flight was ready to take off.

"Ready, set, Europe!" The three of them shouted in excitement.

Daisy went and sat in the corner seat so that she could sleep peacefully. Samuel and Amaya then began their talks. They went on talking, giggling and listening to the music all the way. They reached London just in time.

"Finally! We're over here," Amaya smiled.
"I never knew that London would be this good," Daisy said.
"It has changed a lot. I came here about 8 years ago. It is so well managed and clean as always," Amaya said.
"Now let's go. Amaya, after we get in the taxi, give me the folder which I made regarding the hotel stays," Samuel said.
"Okay," Amaya said.

After that, they went to collect their luggage.

"There. Those bags are ours," Amaya said, pointing toward the bags.

They took their luggage and started moving.

"Oh, Jesus! This is too heavy. My hands are going to break down if I hold

this bag for one more minute," Daisy stopped in between.
"Dora. Just stop being too lazy. You are not a kid anymore," Amaya continued walking.
"But Amay!" Daisy howled.
"Come on Dora," Amaya followed Samuel.
"God!" Daisy commenced walking.
"Good girl," Amaya commented. Amaya wanted to laugh looking at Daisy's condition.
"Let me call the taxi now. You both. Stay here. Ok?" Samuel instructed them because he knew that they were like those girls, who never grew up.

Especially Daisy. Amaya was more mature.

"Amay!" Daisy called up for Amaya showing her teeth. Amaya caught her funny reaction.

"Now what Dora? Tell me what's going on in your harmonious brain," Amaya folded her arms.
"Can I go and get a pizza from the pizza shop out there? I am feeling very hungry" Daisy said.
"No. You are not moving, even a single step from here. Is that clear?" Amaya said.
"Yes, I am going to do that!" Daisy threw the bags on the floor and ran away.
"Why did she just ask me then, if she never wanted to listen? Now, what am I going to do? With these big bags. Ugh," Amaya said to herself.

Then only Samuel came up with the taxi.

"Come on. Let's go?" Samuel hurried but then only noticed that Daisy was missing.
"Where is Daisy now?" he asked.
"She ran to the pizza shop over there," Amaya said.
"And you let her go?" he stared.
"No. I stopped her. But she refused and ran away, saying that she was very hungry,"

They both waited for some time. Till the time Daisy returned, Samuel kept the bags in the taxi with the help of the Driver. They then saw Daisy coming slowly along with the 2 pizza boxes in her hands.

"Wow. What a speed," Amaya murmured.
"Come on fast, we have to leave," Samuel told Daisy.
"You will be charged 1-pound extra sir. This is the waiting charge," The driver told Samuel.

Samuel and Amaya both stared at Daisy with serious faces.

Amaya whispered to Daisy, "Happy?"
Avoiding her, Daisy sarcastically ignored, "Yay, the pizza is so tasty," and then looked around.
"Take yours," Daisy added, handing over the pizza box to Samuel.
"Here," Amaya said, handing over the folder to Samuel.
"Thank God you remembered. I forgot," Samuel said.
"No problem," Amaya said.

He then explained to the driver where to drop them. The driver then turned on the radio station. He turned on the Indian radio station. They got to know that the driver was an Indian too. His name was Vihaan.

"Daisy. Can I ask you something?" Amaya said, turning to Daisy.
"Yeah sure," Daisy said.
"Is Vihaan your brother or something?" Amaya asked.
"Of course not. Why did you ask that?" Daisy took a bite of the pizza.
"Well, the songs he he on his playlist are played by you at home all the time," Amaya said.

The driver laughed. Then Amaya saw Samuel and both started laughing.

Everybody enjoyed her light hearted joke.

"Very funny. Ha ha ha," Daisy said, turning to the other side.

Samuel gave Amaya a clap. 'The Bentley' was the hotel where they were going to stay. It was 2.2 Km from Hyde Park and Kensington Palace. They reached the hotel in about 25 minutes.

Samuel went for the check-in. While Amaya sat on the sofa and waited, Daisy explored the reception. Samuel came in about 15 minutes. They booked a suite.

"This bed will be mine," Daisy said, jumping and diving into the soft mattress.
"Okay," Amaya said.
"And this will be mine," Samuel took the bed in the other room.
"Okay," Amaya said.

Amaya went across the suite to find a bed.

"Hey, where is my bed?" Amaya asked.
"Only two beds are there in our suite," Samuel told her.
"I will sleep with Daisy then," Amaya said.
"No, you cannot sleep with me," Daisy said.
"Why on earth can I not?" Amaya asked.
"Because I have a habit of kicking the person sleeping next to me," Daisy explained.
"So, where am I going to sleep then?" Amaya asked.
"Samuel can share his bed with you," Daisy said, pointing at Samuel.
"Ok?" Samuel said.
"Ok then, I will go with him," Amaya said.

They all slept for some time. Amaya slept the most, for like 4 hours or so. Daisy and Samuel woke up early.

Samuel sat on the bed holding a water bottle in his hands, scrolling on his phone. He kept the bottle aside when he had a gaze at Amaya. He bent and put the hair falling on her face behind her ears. He just got so lost looking at her. She was sleeping peacefully.

"She's beautiful. Isn't she?" Daisy stood near the window.
"Yeah, she is," After a pause, he said, "Astonishingly beautiful.
You accept it or not, you have fallen for her. I can say," Daisy smiled.
"No, I mean, I don't know what's going on in my head," Samuel said.

Amaya hugged him, thinking as if it was the pillow.

"Wow," Daisy laughed watching that.
"This is so romantic," Daisy told him.
"Stop showing as if you don't care. I know everything," she added.
"Oh really?" He spoke.

Amaya woke up. She never noticed what had happened. She saw Daisy's reaction.

"Um, what happened Dora?" Amaya asked, taking a stretch.
"Nothing, if I tell you. You know what I mean," Daisy said.
"Yeah okay. I just asked because of that hilarious reaction you just gave me," Amaya said sleepily.

Amaya got off the bed and went to the balcony.

"This is so amazing," Amaya murmured. The view was ecstatic.
"Here," Samuel said, handing over the coffee to her.
"Thanks," Amaya said.

Amaya took a sip of the coffee.

"Well, this is appreciated. You make it so well. I never knew," Amaya said.
"Well, this is not the first time you commented," He spoke.
"No, it is not like that," Amaya blushed.
"Okay, so do you love somebody?" Samuel hesitantly asked.
"Not yet. Still searching for the one," Amaya gave a 'single but happy' kind of

reaction to him.
"That's impossible. I thought you might be having a boyfriend," He acted as if he did not know.
"Not at all. Who is going to be happy to date a girl like me? I mean I am not smart, or special. Everyone bullied me in high school in India. They called me a 'big fat nuthead'," Amaya shyly said.
"Get those freaks the hell out of your head. Those brats must be jealous of you. I mean how could they even think of you like that!" Samuel got angry.
"Whoa. Are you angry?" Amaya asked.
"If someone was to date me, he would have by now. Even if later, I am sure there would some guy out there. I am sure there would be some guy out there," Amaya added.
"I will," Samuel murmured.
"What did you just say?" Amaya sipped the coffee.
"Nothing. I mean. I have to go and get dressed for exploring London tonight, Yeah. I also should probably get ready. By the way, where are we going?" Amaya asked.
"It's a surprise," He ran in.

Amaya understood what he just murmured. She was sort of happy about it but she didn't know why. Her stomach was all butterfly.

AFTER 1 HOUR

"Hey Dora, are you still lying on the couch? Come on. Go get ready," Amaya said loudly.
"No, who told you that I was coming?" Daisy said.
"Aren't you joining us tonight?" Amaya asked.
"Who told you I was going to join? It's you who have to go on the date with Sam and not me. Okay," Daisy said.
"What? Is it a date?" Amaya was confused.
"Yeah," Daisy said.
"Oh okay, tell me how am I looking?" Amaya was wearing a beautiful black dress.

"You look gorgeous Amy! I wished that I was just as beautiful as you," Daisy said.
"No Daisy, we both are sisters and we are always the same. But I may say that you are more beautiful than me," Amaya told her.
"Aww Really? Come here," Daisy gave Amaya a tight hug. "You know what? You are going to kill it tonight. Every beautiful personality out there will not be even comparable to you. You look that pretty. And if it is about Sam then, he's going to be into you tonight. He's going to love it," she added.
"I just want to see his face then ha-ha," Amaya giggled.
"Me too," Daisy said.

Samuel came out of the room. He looked handsome. But just after he got a look at Amaya, he was stunned.

"You look," Samuel's mouth was still open.
"Stunningly gorgeous," he added.
"You too look very handsome today, I must say," Amaya gave a smile to him.

Samuel was so stunned by her beauty that he wanted to hug her and tell her how much he loved her. But he couldn't do so.

"Are you ready to go?" he asked.
"Yes. Let's go," Amaya said.
"May I?" he held her hand and they went out together.
"So where are we going? Can you tell me?" Amaya asked while walking through the lobby.
"You'll get to know," Samuel opened the door of the car. He booked a limousine for both of them that night.
"Okay, that means I have to wait a little more I guess," Amaya said.
"Yes," Samuel entered the car.

Amaya was so excited to know what the plans were for the night. The moment they reached there he closed her eyes, covering them with both his hands.

"Sam," Amaya said.
"Wait a second," Samuel said.
"Now, you may open your eyes," Samuel told her.
"This is so beautiful," Amaya went speechless watching that place's beauty.
"So, madam, here we are. This is," Samuel was speaking when.
"River Thames luxury dinner cruise. I know. My father brought my mother here," Amaya said, feeling happy.
"This is a dream come true. I always wanted someone to bring me here. And today my dream came true. Thank you, Samuel," Amaya hugged him.
"It's a pleasure to bring you here Amaya. Now, shall we?" Samuel and Amaya headed in.
"Sir, you came to the very right place. Tonight, you are going to enjoy the finest jazz band. And we have our very special and delicious 3-course meal. The Chi jazz quintet will perform a range of cool, ambient jazz tunes and many more. Also, very importantly, you have to admire the world-famous London sights out here," a person standing at the entrance told them.

They both got seated soon. The jazz program was about to start any minute.

"Eating and listening to light music feels so good," Amaya said.
"Let us order some wine," Samuel suggested.
"Yes, we probably should," Amaya said.

The music made them feel calm.

"The aura here is kind of romantic," Amaya told him.
"No doubt. It is," Samuel said.
"Your wine sir," the waiter served.
"Thank you so much," Amaya said.
"Cheers!" both brought their glasses up in the air.
"Want to Dance?" Samuel popped up the question.
"I would love to," Amaya said, taking his hand and walking to the dance floor.

They both started dancing alongside other couples.

A man there stood up and gave a shout-out, "To all the couples out there!" "To all the couples out here!" Everyone repeated and raised their glasses.

Amaya had a feeling of 'pure love' somewhere deep inside her. But she still did not know what she felt about Samuel. She surely liked him but wasn't sure of 'LOVE'.

Their love was reflected as they danced together.

Soon, they went back and sat down. On their way, a lady stopped them to let them know how beautiful they looked together.

"Thank you," Amaya smiled looking at Samuel.

Samuel welcomed her with a smile. Their special cuisine had already been served.

"This food is exotic," Amaya said.
"It's very delicious," Samuel said.
"So, what do you think of that girl standing over there?" Amaya asked.
"Which one?" Samuel asked.
"Standing near to the stage. The one in the yellow dress," She spoke.
"That one. She looks absurd to me. I mean, look how hard she is trying to get that boy's attention, who's not even interested," he spoke.

They both started laughing at the weird reactions of that girl. Both were done with eating.

"Let's go outside. Admiring the place in real life is better than watching it from the window," Amaya stood up and pulled Samuel's hand.
"Okay. Let's go," He removed the white cloth from his neck.

The sky seemed so peaceful. The stars were shining so bright that they looked just like a true picture of heaven. They both stood in one corner of the outer deck.

The London lights sparkled in their eyes.

"I never knew how this place was when my father brought my mother over here. It's a heart-touching view. I mean, this is as mesmerizing as it looks in all the pictures on Google. My father never clicked any pictures of this place. He just kept these images in his mind. He never told me what his experience was. I never stopped guessing though. I am just so speechless at this particular point in time," Amaya expressed all her happiness with her words. She was so thankful to Samuel.

"Was there anyone you had in your life before?" She asked.

"No. I am not a guy of those funky kinds of girls. I need a loyal and delicate one," Samuel said.

"So, why is the order still hung up?" Amaya asked, giving a thoughtful look.

"Order?" he asked.

"Yeah. Order; the one you have made to 'The God's Bazaar' but not yet shipped to you," she spoke.

"Oh, man. You are crazy," he burst out in laughter.

"Yes, I am. No doubt," she giggled.

"You will surely get someone soon," she glanced towards the sky.

"Really? How do you know that? Well, is that you?" He said giggling.

"Oh, come on. Shut up. I was just making a guess. There must be some girl whom you like or 'love'," she guessed.

"Yes," Samuel said.

"Who?" she gave him a surprised look.

"You," he murmured.

"Huh?" She was confused.

"Uh, um you know that I don't know who that is going to be," he somewhat said.

"You know what? I never want to go back from here," Amaya faced towards the sky. "This place is so charming. It is magnificent," she added.

"Me too. I just want to stay here exploring the stars all night. But unfortunately, time is passing by. It is running like a horse. We have only one? 6 minutes exactly now," he checked his watch.

"Well. What can I say, Sam? I am so grateful to you for bringing me over

here. Thank you for such a pleasant night," she held his hand and expressed her thankfulness.
"How many times are you going to thank me now?" He asked.
"Many more times. This is not enough," she smiled.

He came near her and hugged her tightly. She could feel all of the love in his arms. She knew about her falling for him, truly. They both danced together in the streets. They reached the hotel by 11 at night. Everything just made their day. They both were very happy about it.

DAY-2

"Amay! Wake up!" Daisy screamed as the sun came out.

Both Amaya and Samuel were sleeping. Rather deep sleeping. They both were actually in each other's arms, which they didn't know. At all!

"Oh god. These two are so in love with each other. Though they look so cute," Daisy spoke.
"I think they drank extra last night. But, I am the most excited to know what happened last night," She added. Daisy got crazy and went to bring water. She threw all of the jug's water on them.
"Ay!" Amaya screamed.
"Who is this idiot? Playing with. W-water!" she added.

Amaya got up and so did Samuel. But Amaya's hair got stuck in Samuel's bracelet which he wore.

"Ouch"
"Oh that," Samuel helped her out.
"This duo is too cute," Daisy murmured.
"Daisy, did you just say something?" Amaya untangled her hair.
"No Amaya. You would have misheard something. And for your kind information, I have been trying to wake you both up for so long," Daisy said,

showing her watch to them.

Samuel and Amaya suddenly got lost in each other's eyes. Their eyes were full of love.

"Uhm-uhm," Daisy attracted their attention.

Amaya rushed off the bed. "But it's only 7 now,"
"But we also have to go out and have some fun. Isn't it?" Daisy acted innocent.
"Okay- okay. Don't give me those looks now. Let's go, get ready," Amaya got off the bed.

Daisy smiled wide and went out on the balcony. Amaya got off the bed and went to get freshened up. Meanwhile, Samuel watched television.

"Hey! You there, Hi!" Daisy screamed on the balcony. The juice in Samuel's hand slipped off.
"Oh shit!" Samuel shouted. He went towards the balcony.
"What the hell is happening to you Daisy?" He shouted.
"Oh, actually I. I just saw that cute guy out there and so I was just having some fun, that's it. Hey, who are you? Handsome stranger guy? Tell me something about yourself," She screamed trying to flirt again.
"Whoa! Have you completely lost it?" Samuel said.
"I had already lost it when I landed on a place called 'Earth'," She was being silly.
"Gosh! This women is mad," he said and went inside.

Meanwhile, Daisy continued to talk to that stranger.

"I am Adam! And what about you? Beautiful lady?"
"My name is Daisy,"

Amaya came out till then.

"You know what? Your best friend has gone nuts!" Samuel said.

"Oh God, what did she do now?" she asked.

"I don't know. Go look for yourself," he said and went to get fresh.

"This girl is crazy!" Amaya looked out for Daisy.

"Dora? Dora? Do...," She paused and saw Daisy in the Balcony.

"Would you like to be my boyfriend?" Daisy said.

"Woah what! Daisy!! What on earth is going on huh?" Amaya shouted.

"Get in. Get in right now!"

"What? No! I'm still talking to this cute guy," Daisy said.

"That's not a cute guy but rather a stranger. Come on, get in," Amaya pulled Daisy in.

"Yeah?" The stranger shouted in the middle of the street.

"Have you gone completely insane? I mean, what can I just say? What has gone into you? I just can't imagine the way you are behaving right now. Ugh!!" Amaya yelled.

"Calm down Amay! Just calm down," Daisy said.

"How can I just calm down huh? You are doing silly things and i should just keep watching and applaud ? You only tell me what kind of behaviour is that? You are talking to some stranger guy and in fact, flirting with him. No, wait, asking him out? And you want me to calm down. Are you of this planet only or have you just come from Pluto?" Amaya burst out in anger.

"But Amay since he was cute, I just could not control my emotions," Daisy said.

"What do you mean by 'could not'? You should be able to control your unusual exciteful emotions. This is reality and not a film going on. We don't even know that person, don't know what he does or what his name is!" Amaya said.

"Actually, Adam is his name," he interrupted.

"You are not supposed to talk to some stranger. You don't even know him. Maybe he is a smuggler or maybe he is a person doing some illegal business!" Amaya said.

"Oh really? A smuggler in a suit? I never knew that smugglers or bad businessmen also wore suits," Daisy raised her eyebrow. And I know him.

"How come?"

Let me show you.

"Hey, Adam!" she spoke in a flirty tone.
"Hey, Daisy!" he replied.
"Well, no one knows!" Amaya was baffled.

Amaya and Daisy went crazy while fighting.

"Girls. Girls. Just stop it! What the hell is going on? This is not a circus. This is also not our home. This is a hotel ok! So just stop it," Samuel came out of the bathroom. He was so irritated that he had to come out in a towel.
"Eesh!!" Both the girls saw him and looked away.
"What? Never saw a man in a towel before? What are you, Jimmy Choo?" he said.
"Just shut up!" Both the girls shouted together.
"Go and wear something and then speak to us, ok?" they screamed.
"Okay. Cool down man," he spoke.
"Insane!" Daisy whispered.
"Did you just say something?" Amaya asked.
"No, not at all Amay," She went to watch some television.
"What? Are you going to watch television now? Not in the mood to bathe or what?" Amaya switched off the TV.

Samuel came out in his outfit this time.

"Thank God!" Amaya said.
"What?" Samuel said.
"Nothing," she said.
"Fine!" He went out in the balcony.

And then only he saw that same person with whom Daisy was flirting. He was still standing near the hotel entrance.

"This guy is mad too," He thought.
"Amay!" he called out to Amaya.

"What?" she came running.
"Look at that guy," Samuel pointed towards Adam.
"What guy?" Amaya got confused.
"See that," He tilted her face towards Adam.
"Shoot! This person is still over here. God! What is happening today?" Amaya said.
"Are you just going to look at that guy?" he asked.
"Now, what am I supposed to do then?" Amaya slowly screamed.
"We should think what should be done to get him out of here," he screamed in a low tone.
"Right!" Amaya started to think of some ideas.
"But what should we do now? Let me think," she scratched her head in confusion.
"Idea!" Amaya exclaimed.
"Tell me what the idea is. Fast," he asked.
"Look what we are going to do is, tell him that Daisy called him in the nearby garden now. So that he at least leaves for now," she clicked her fingers.
"You are a good girl. Okay then, let's do this thing," both of them clapped hands.

They called Adam.

"Hey! You there. Daisy has gone to the nearby garden. She called you too. Go meet her over there," Samuel pointed towards the garden's lane.
"What? I never saw her go," Adam said.
"B-But," Samuel was confused about what was to be said now.
"Because she used the other way. Okay now. Just go," Amaya covered for him.
"She would be waiting for you," Samuel said.
"Is there some other way too?" Adam mysteriously questioned.
"I told you that there is no time for questions right now. Could you please go now or she will go away?" Amaya gave a wide fake smile.

Adam took his scooter and went away. Daisy came out with her hair messed up.

"Where is my hairbrush?!" Daisy shouted in anger.
"Oh-k. I got it," Daisy added as it was lying on the floor.
"How careless is she?" Samuel said.
"Since childhood. She's still the same. She has not even changed a bit. But I may say she is perfect in everything. You know what? Back when we were 11 she had lost the most favourite thing she owned, her doll,"
"What? She was 11 and still played with dolls!" Sam said.
"Yeah. But don't shout she's going to kill us both," she kept her hand on his mouth.
"So, where was I?" Amaya continued.
"The doll," Samuel said.
"Yeah, she was looking for the doll almost all day. When she found the doll, her face was horrible," Amaya spoke.
"Why?" Samuel questioned.
"Because the doll had been washed in the washing machine in which she threw it at night and because of which one eye of the doll went missing and the nose got torn out," she and Samuel both burst into laughter.
"Like seriously, how pathetically careless is she? Oh my," he could not control his laughter.
"Correct," Amaya couldn't control her laughter.
"Wow! Is there something funny going on over here? You can share that with me too," Daisy jumped beside them.
"Yeah, the doll.," Samuel's tongue slipped.
"What doll?" Daisy stared at both of them.
"Oh- nothing, not the doll," Amaya said.
"Then what?" Daisy asked.
"Th-the ball! Yes! A ball just came and hit him hard on his head ha-ha. Right, Sam?" Amaya winked at Samuel.
"What? Oh yeah, it hit me right over here," Samuel said, pointing at the edge of his head.
"Okay. So, you got hurt?" Daisy brushed her hair.
"Yeah. Ouch," Samuel was a very pathetic actor.
"So why are you laughing huh?" Daisy folded her arms.

They all gave each other a strange look.

"Tell me now, what the matter is," she asked.
"The matter is that he is mad. Now let's change the topic and decide where we are going," Amaya said.
"Well, that's already decided," Samuel said.
"Then tell us," Amaya said.
"No, I am not," he said.
"What do you mean you are not? You have to. We have not come here to see these surprises. We too need to know the plans for the trips I guess?" Amaya said.
"No," Samuel ran to pick up his bag-pack and the DSLR with which he ran outside the room.
"What is happening today?" Amaya banged her foot on the floor.
"Madness," Daisy left.

Soon after, Amaya joined them both in the taxi.

"Driver, would you mind if I just played some of my songs here?" Daisy asked the driver with a wide smile on her face.
"No prob..." The driver was speaking when Amaya spoke,
"Yes. Yes, there is a problem,"
"Why?" Daisy asked.
"Because he has to focus on the traffic out there and he may get distracted because of your songs," Amaya said.
"But madam," Driver said.
"Shut up!" Amaya said.

Samuel gave a funny laugh.

"Fine," Daisy looked out of the window. Amaya and Daisy slept in the car. Samuel took out his whistle and started blowing it.

"Who's this idiot?" Daisy said with her eyes closed.
"Stop it!" Amaya shouted.
"It seems that someone's not interested in having some fun," Samuel said.

Then both the girls jumped off excitedly.
"Ta-da. Here we are, ladies," Samuel said.

Daisy opened the window and put her head out.

"Wow! This is amazing," She then walked out.
"This is so pretty," Amaya said.

Buckingham Palace! The place which Daisy wanted to see for ages.

Samuel had already hired a guide for their Europe trip.

"Where is this man?" Samuel saw his watch.
"Who?" Daisy asked.
"The guide. I hired one and he is late already," He spoke.
"Hello, hello sir!" The guide said.
"Michael?" Samuel asked.
"Yes sir. Extremely sorry for being late. I will be guiding you in Europe from today, he spoke.
"Okay then, let's start. Amaya come, let's go," Samuel waved.
"Yes, I am coming," she said.

Amaya was busy clicking pictures of Buckingham Palace.

"Follow me," Michael started walking.

Amaya was still busy taking pictures of the palace. Samuel went beside her and asked her if she was interested in going ahead. He held her hand and started walking as Amaya was not listening to him.

"It will seem to be a little boring as I guide you and tell you things but don't worry, we'll have loads of fun together," Michael continued to walk.
"Buckingham Palace is the London residence and administrative headquarters of the monarch of the UK. This place is often the Centre of state occasions and royal hospitality. Originally known as Buckingham Palace, the building

at the core of today's palace was a large townhouse built for the Duke of Buckingham in 1703 on a site that had been in private ownership for at least 150 years"

"So, now we have to listen to this?" Daisy took out her camera.

"Unfortunately, yes. Otherwise, how would you get to know this place? So, now we have reached the entrance of the palace and you can click the pictures", Daisy and Amaya started to click pictures.

"Hey Sam, if you don't mind, could you click a picture of us?" Daisy handed the camera to Samuel.

"Yeah sure," Samuel took the camera.

"You look pretty good today, Daisy," Amaya gave a wink while posing for the picture.

"Really? Well, should I take it as a compliment then?"

"Yes. You can for sure,"

Both the girls posed for the picture.

"Well, how many more huh? 10 pictures at the same spot already. There are so many more spots," Samuel gave a tiring look.

"Looks like someone's tired already," Amaya and Daisy laughed out loud.

"You think it's funny?"

"Well yes!" both continued to laugh.

CHAPTER NINE

"Doctor! How's he doing? Please tell doctor. How's he now? Any response? Doctor, why aren't you replying?" Amaya was in tears.
"Calm down Amaya. He'll be alright," Daisy held her shoulders, giving support.

What happened exactly that day? So, let's go back for a while.

DAY-3

"It has been a long day. I'm so tired," Amaya sat on the bench.
"Amay me too," Daisy jumped and sat next to her.
"Let me go and fetch some water and ice creams," Samuel said and as he was crossing the road he got hit by a truck.
"Amayaaaa!" He shouted.

Both Amaya and Daisy hurried towards him.

"Sam! Sam! Open your eyes, Sam. Open your eyes. Please open them up!" Amaya hugged Samuel in her arms and cried.

The blood streamed down the road through his body.

"Ambulance! Someone please, call the ambulance!" Daisy shouted.

IN THE HOSPITAL

He was taken to St. Mary's Hospital quickly. The doctors and the nurses rushed towards the ICU. Daisy held Amaya. "Everything is going to be fine," Amaya cried.

"Hello? Ma'am," Amaya called his mom.

"Oh, hello Amaya. How are you all? Is the trip going fine? I hope you are all enjoying it to the fullest," Ms. Russell responded.

Amaya was in tears informing her about the accident. Ms. Russell went numb.

"I'll be there by tonight. Don't worry Amaya," Ms. Russell cut the call and hurried.

After 4 hours of the operation, the doctors came out of the ICU. It was 8PM then. Ms. Russell was to reach by 9PM.

"Amaya? The doctors are here," Daisy told Amaya. Amaya rushed towards the doctors.

"Follow me to my cabin please," Dr. Steward was in charge of Samuel's case.

"You are?" the doctor asked.

"Samuel's colleague," Amaya said.

"Do you live in London only?" the doctor asked.

"Well no. Actually, we came here on a tour," she kept her hands on the table.

"Ok. Well Miss. I need you to know that you all have to make some arrangements for staying up here," Before he could finish, Amaya interrupted.

"Yeah, we have made them," she responded.

"But not for a few days. A few months or maybe," After a long pause.

"I don't really know," He continued.

"But why? What's wrong with him? He is going to be fine right?" Amaya interrupted.

"Yes, he is but," Again, a long pause by the doctor.

"But? But what doctor?" Amaya got tense.

"My dear, your friend Samuel is in a coma," His head is severely injured and his condition, for the time being, is critical, so you have to look upon who will stay up here in London with him," Amaya burst into tears.

"He'll take time. I can understand your feelings, my dear. We will keep on

monitoring your friend. He is going to be fine," he sympathetically said.
"I hope so," Amaya left the doctor's cabin.

Ms. Russell was there finally.

"Amaya, baby what does the doctor say?" She was worried.

Amaya told her everything that the doctor told them and hugged her.

"Who's the patient's relative?" a nurse showed up. Ms. Russell took a step forward.
"Ma'am, you need to fill up the form at the reception," she said and went towards the doctor's cabin. Ms. Russell went to the reception.

Meanwhile, Daisy went to bring some coffee and snacks from the hospital canteen.

"What is happening? I can't see him like this. In this condition. How can God be so cruel? Ugh! What is happening? I just don't know how to react. He's so, I mean he's so nice, a human with a loving personality. I mean, why him God? You should've chosen me instead. Why?" Amaya's thoughts weren't stopping. She sat in disgust. She felt as if her heart was injured and not Samuel.

She was so confused about her feelings for him.

Daisy came up with some coffee and burgers. She handed a coffee and a burger to Amaya. Ms. Russell came and sat next to Amaya. They all were in a traumatic situation then. They sat still and ate quietly. After an hour Daisy and Amaya went outside to get some fresh air. Ms. Russell slept sitting in a chair. She was very exhausted.

"I never thought a situation like this would occur," Amaya was so much in shock that she wasn't even able to express herself properly in front of Daisy.
"Yeah, me too," Daisy walked along with Amaya.

They both went and sat on the porch area outside.

Looking at the stars, Amaya got lost into her thoughts. Nobody knew what she was thinking.

"You love him, don't you?" Daisy said looking into her eyes.
"What? Oh no," Amaya said.
"You are lying Amaya. You yourself don't know about this; you know that. Very well," Daisy politely smiled.
"No. I mean. Like. I don't..., I don't really know," Amaya was just looking at those twinkling stars in the night sky.
"You don't know but your heart does. And also, you don't speak but your eyes do speak sweetie," Daisy smiled.
"Um. I don't know. I never knew that I would meet someone in such a hurry and get this much attached to that person. I remember the first time we met, he literally looked like a flirty type but I never knew that he would be this humble and have such a generous personality. He took me out for dinner and that too to one of my most admired places," Amaya said.
"That is known as a date and not dinner," Daisy giggled.
"What? No," Amaya pushed her shoulder.
"Yes, it was baby," Daisy answered.
Both of them laughed.

"But who knew we would end up seeing this day," Amaya went silent.
"It's already midnight honey. I think we should go and sleep," Daisy stood up.
"Yeah. We probably should," Amaya got lost in her thoughts yet again.
"Ok now stop thinking too much and let's go in. Everything's going to be alright, I'm sure," Daisy held Amaya's hand and both of them went inside the hospital.

CHAPTER TEN

A month had passed by but Samuel was hospitalized. But his condition was so critical that he hadn't come out of the coma yet.

Daisy had left for India 10 days back due to some urgency. She had to finish up some of her Indian property matters.

Amaya and Ms. Russell were still there for Samuel.

Amaya brought up the medicines and food every single time. She never let Ms. Russell panic.

Every single minute was suspicious for them.

The doctors still weren't able to identify the time span Samuel is going to take to recover.

"Any response doctors?" Ms. Russell rushed. Dr. Steward nodded in negative and left towards the cabin. Everybody was praying for Samuel's speedy recovery.
"Amaya?" Ms. Russell brought some tea.

They were sitting outside the doctor's cabin. She gave a smile to her.

"Thank you for being there all the time with us honey. I am so grateful to you Amaya for saving my son's life. You have not only proved to be a hardworking colleague but also a pure soul. I can't thank you enough baby," Ms. Russell gave a smile.
"No need to thank me ma'am. Thank God for saving him and letting him

survive," Amaya held her hands.
"Then too sweetie, I just can't thank you enough," Ms. Russell smiled.

After having a cup of tea, they went inside the doctor's cabin.

"Ms. Russell, we are going to shift your son to ward no. 16. We'll keep a check on him, whether he responds or not because according to me his brain has recovered a bit," the doctor said.
"And yes, Ms. Russell, you will need to fill this form. It will give us some idea about the patient's details. He needs some blood because of major blood loss," The doctor handed over the form to her.

They then left his cabin.

"Let me fill this up. Till then you can book the cab," Ms. Russell.

"Ok. I'll go book a cab," Amaya left.

Ms. Russell started filling the form. After half an hour they left. It was already late in the evening. They went and had their dinner in the hotel.

It was 3:00 AM when Amaya woke up all of a sudden. Looking outside the window, thoughts ran through her mind.

"Why? Why did this happen? Why wasn't I there and not him? Why do I feel so attached to him? Do I, do I love him?" Tears streamed down her eyes.

CHAPTER ELEVEN

At around 7 in the morning when Ms. Russell's phone rang.

"Hello?" Ms. Russell answered.

She immediately, after cutting the call, woke Amaya up.

"Amy? Sweetie? Wake up fast!" she tapped her hand on her shoulder.
"What happened?" Amaya rubbed her eyes.
"Sweetie, the doctor just called. He told me we need to reach the hospital really quickly. Sam just responded. He just came out of the coma," Ms. Russell smiled.
"That's such great news. Thank God!" Amaya stood up in excitement.
"I know right? Go get ready honey. I'll arrange a cab till then," Ms. Russell went to the balcony.
"Okay," Amaya rushed.

After about 30 minutes, both were ready and hurried.

AT THE HOSPITAL

"Ms. Russell, I'm really very happy to tell you about Mr. Samuel's health right now. It's surely a God's miracle. In most of the cases like Samuel, the patients take many years to recover or even come back to their senses. But Samuel did it within a year and that too in such a short span of time. You can check over him but do not offer him any sort of heavy diet for the time being. We'll be making a special diet plan for him since we need to give extra attention to him," the doctor gave a smile.

They both left the doctor's cabin and rushed to see Samuel. Ms. Russell hugged him tight just as she entered the room.

"There he is," Amaya thought of wiping off the tear in her eye and smiled whole-heartedly.
"Hey," she stepped forward and held his hand.
"You'll be okay," she whispered looking into his eyes.
"So, how do you feel, madam?" the doctor entered the ward.
"I really feel so blessed right now," tears rolled down his mother's eyes.

Amaya stayed with him while Ms. Russell went to fetch some of the stuff from the hotel. She sat right next to him looking into his eyes all the time.

Both of them were so lost looking into each other's eyes that they never got to know when it was 4 in the evening.

The doctor came to check Samuel. "Well, how do you feel, hero?" "Weak. Useless," he spoke.
"Not useless!" Amaya interrupted.
"You aren't useless Sam! You're strong and brave," she added.
"She's right. You really have that strength to recover really fast. Keep that in mind kid," meanwhile the doctor checked his pulse.
"Just never ever give up Sam," Amaya added, holding his hand. "Alright then, let me just go and send the nurse along with his food," It was 9 PM when Amaya's phone rang.
"Hey sweetie, would you mind if you stayed with Samuel during the nights? I really have to finish off the pending magazine projects and attend the meeting along with our new partners," Ms. Russell asked in a worried tone.
"You really don't need to ask for it. I'll surely stay with him," Amaya stood beside the door.
"Thank you so much sweetie," Ms. Russell thereafter cut the call.

After talking to Ms. Russell Amaya went and stood near the window staring outside, having several thoughts run through her mind.

Looking towards the sky she thought, "I feel incomplete. I don't know why but yes; I feel a lot messed up right now. There is something that I'm not able to figure out. A feeling maybe, that my heart's trying to tell me in all ways but my mind can't understand it,"
"Haven't slept yet?" Samuel's voice came from behind. He was awake.

"Um, not yet," she answered.
"Why not? It's already so late. You should rest now,"
"Yeah. I'm just not able to sleep right now," Amaya turned back, facing him.
"Why not?" he sat, resting his back.
"I don't know," She hesitantly answered.
"Come here. Sit with me," Samuel patted the bed. She went and sat beside him.
"Tell me about it," she said.
"About what?" She was worried.
"The thing that's making you feel uncomfortable," he continued.
"I don't know. What's in my mind right now? I'm just so blank," she stared outside the window.
He held her hand. "Listen, whatever you feel right now is just temporary. You don't need to worry about it. Just take a deep breath and relax. I'm always here for you,"

She gave him a smile and hugged him.

"Thank you for being there," Amaya smiled.
"Always," he calmly hugged her back.

CHAPTER TWELVE

Ms. Russell reached the hospital by 9 in the morning.

"Hey, Sweeties?" The moment she entered Samuel's room she saw that both were sleeping holding hands. Amaya rested her head beside Samuel. She dozed off sitting in the chair.

"Honey?" she brushed her hair gently with her hands, waking her up.

Amaya woke up.

"Ms. Russell? Good morning. Um, what time is it?"

"Good morning sweetie. It's 9:10 right now. You must go to the hotel and rest for a while. Come by the evening,"

"Okay. Yeah, I must go and get ready," She left the room.

Amaya booked a cab and went straight to the hotel. After freshening up she made herself a cup of coffee. She went and stood on the balcony along with the coffee.

"I guess I should visit the church today," Ms. Russell told me to visit the Westminster Cathedral once.

AT THE HOSPITAL

Samuel called up for Amaya. The doctor came in instead.

"What happened dear? Any issue?" he asked.

"Um, no doctor. I was just looking for the girl who stays with me," Samuel wondered where Amaya was.

"Oh, you are talking about Amaya?" the doctor peeped into the file in his hands.

"Yes. Where is she? I can't see her anywhere," He started looking here and there.

"She has gone to the hotel Sam," Ms. Russel entered his room.

"Till when will she be back mom?" Samuel asked. "I don't really know. I guess most probably by the evening,"

"Oh. Okay," Samuel bent his face in disappointment.

"Should I give her your message, if you want?" Ms. Russell kept hand over his shoulder.

"Oh, no need Mom, it's fine," Samuel gave a smile.

"Let me bring something for you to eat then," "No, it's fine. Am full right now. I must rest now,"

"Okay then," both the doctor and Ms. Russell left.

"Samuel laid down and tried sleeping,"

AT THE HOTEL

On the other hand, in the hotel, Amaya was getting ready to go to the church.

She wore a full-sleeved white top along with a sober long cream-coloured coat and denim leggings. Picking up her bag, she rushed towards the door. She booked the cab while in the hallway. The cab arrived within the next 5 minutes.

IN THE CHURCH

The church was not so crowded that day. She proceeded and sat down in the corner of the first row.

"Jesus. My lord, how do I thank you enough for making Samuel come back to his senses? I have no words to describe my respect and love for you right now. I am at a loss for words. I don't know, but I feel as if I have some sort of feelings for him, somewhere in my heart. I have never felt like this before for any guy. He has done so many things for me in such a short time. We have been able to build a strong bond with each other in no time. I just do not know what my feelings exactly are right now for him. There is something that I feel my heart knows very well, but my mind does not. I just want you to bless him with good health and a speedy recovery. I want him to be happy," a tear rolled down Amaya's eyes.

Wiping the tears, she got up and smiled. The people started to gather. Father came near her and told her, "Don't worry my child. God has brought you to this Church for a reason. Whatever you want, he shall give you for sure," "I hope so, father,"
"God bless you my child", he kept his hand on her head.

The prayer started after 20 minutes. After 2 hours, Amaya left for the hotel. It was already 3 PM then.

"I'm so exhausted now. I'll straight away go to bed, once I reach," Amaya thought.

She dozed off to sleep as soon as she entered her room. It was 7 PM when her phone rang.

"Hello?"
"Amy? Baby where are you? Have been waiting for you for so long. I thought you were coming by the evening," Ms. Russell was there on the other side.
"Oh! Oh my God. What time is it?" Amaya jumped up and stood up.
"It's 7 PM already love," Ms. Russell looked at the clock.
"I'm coming right away. I'm so sorry, I dozed off,"
"It's okay sweetie. Come fast,"

Amaya cut the call and hurried. She combed her hair, picked up her bag and locked the door. She booked the cab for the hospital.

"Ma'am, there's a lot of traffic over here. It'll take us some time to reach the hospital," the driver said.
"Oh no! It's okay. You proceed," Amaya texted Ms. Russel about the heavy traffic on the way.

She stared outside the window, plugged in the lead and played some music. Samuel started reading a book, by the time Amaya reached. It was 10 at night till she reached.

"Oh gosh, what an exhausting day it was," Amaya shut the car door.

By the time she reached Samuel's room, he was already asleep.

Ms. Russell had also left 15 minutes past Amaya. Amaya sat on the sofa, all exhausted. She took out her phone, exploring 30 work mails.

"Oh God!" She took a deep breath looking at a load of office work.

She took out her laptop from the bag and started working.

Amaya was a very responsible girl. She never kept any of her work pending.
"Need some water?" Samuel stood beside her.

It was 3 AM in the morning.

"Oh, Sam, why did you get up? Go to bed, right now!" She stood up worriedly.
"It's ok Amy," he smiled.
"No, it's not," She took him towards the bed.
"You're not all ok right now Sam. Do not forget that," she added.
"I know Amy,"
"No, you don't!" She held his shoulders and made him sit down.
"Calm down. Relax!"
"No, I won't. You are not well right now and I'll make sure, you don't mess up, okay,"

"Fine! Fine," he raised his hands in surrender.
"Now, drink some water, you workaholic," he added.
"Alright," she drank some water. "But do not repeat this again,"
"Fine. And why on earth are you still awake? You can complete the office work in the morning too,"
"I know but this needs to be done by tomorrow and it's way too much work," Amaya took a deep breath.
"You could have woken up early?"
"I know but I can't. I am just too lazy to wake up so early,"
"Great then. Now just shut off your laptop and kindly sleep," she said pointing towards the laptop.
"Just 30 more minutes please?" she made a pleading face.
"No chance. Just do what is being told to you. Right now!"
"Fine," she shut down her laptop and took two sips of water.

She pulled in the curtains by the window, after which laid on the sofa, pulling over the blanket.

"Good night, Amaya,"
"Good night, Sam. I'm in no mood to sleep," she huffed.
"What? Are you an owl or something? Come on, sleep now," he stared at her.
"Okay!" she spoke.
"Good," he closed his eyes.

It was already 3:30 AM when both dozed off to sleep.

CHAPTER THIRTEEN

It was already 9 AM in the morning. Everyone was awake, instead of Amaya. She was asleep peacefully. Samuel was having his breakfast. After having his breakfast, he called up for the nurse and asked for Amaya's bag. He took out her laptop and started working on it. His left arm was still not alright. He wanted to help her by finishing with the work that she had got the previous night.

By 11 AM he finished up with her work.

Amaya woke up by 11:30 AM.

"Good morning," Samuel sipped his coffee.
"Good morning," Amaya yawned.
"Oh my God! What time is it?" she jumped off the sofa.
"It's 11:30 AM. So, you're finally up huh," "I'm but, my work!" she got tense. She quickly took out her laptop.

"My work. Huh? It's done. How is this even possible?"
"Who did that?"
"Uh-huh, I did that. You do not need to thank me at all, okay,"
"What? But why? How can you do my work?" she screamed politely.
"What do you mean by that? Why can't I?"
"No, you can't! Last night too, you got scolded by me for the same thing. I told you not to do any work at all!"
"And why is that?" he sat up straight.
"Because your health is not perfectly fine. You aren't allowed to do anything,"
"Since your work is done now, kindly keep silent, Miss Workaholic"
"Why do you keep calling me that?"

"Because you are a workaholic, Miss Amaya,"
"No, I'm not!"
"Yes, you are. Workaholic,"
"Hello, Salaam, Namaste! This is Daisy reporting here!" Daisy entered the room with joyous energy.
"Daisy! Oh my. Come here give me a hug,"

Amaya and Daisy tightly hugged each other.

"What a surprise Dora! It feels so good to see you after so long. By the way, you were going to come in December this year. It's only August," "Yeah, I was going to but one of my relatives had a wedding so, I had to.
"Well, that's great," Amaya smiled.
"Hey, Sam! My ears were blessed to hear about your recovery," Daisy gave a bouquet to him.
"Yeah, thank you for the flowers though," he said, keeping the flowers aside.

The nurse came in to check on Samuel.

"These two tablets have to be given to him right now," she said, handing over the tablets to Amaya.
"Okay,"

Amaya handed over the tablets along with a glass of water to Samuel.

"Here,"
"Thank you, Miss Workaholic," he said, taking his medicine.
"Stop it now Sam," She laughed annoyed.
"You both still fight on little things?" Daisy laughed.
"Why not? We always do," Samuel laughed.
"Yes, because he unnecessarily tries to annoy me ha-ha," Amaya looked at Samuel annoyed.
"You guys are just impossible," Daisy continued laughing.

The doctor came in to check on Samuel.

Meanwhile, Daisy and Amaya went to the café and had coffee.

"We need to perform a small examination on Samuel, just to keep a check on his recovery. If he responds in an affirmative way, then chances are that we can discharge him soon," Doctor told Amaya.
"That's great news doctor," Amaya felt extremely happy.

Amaya straightaway called Ms. Russell to give her the good news too. The whole day passed by examining Samuel.

Amaya and Daisy later on, slept on the sofa in his room. All of them were very exhausted that day so they slept early by 10 PM.

CHAPTER FOURTEEN

It was a month after, when Samuel was finally ready to go home. Everyone was very happy.

"20th of September, finally you'll be getting to go back home Sam," Amaya stood by Samuel.
"It feels as if I have got a new life to live. A chance to live again. I can't be thankful enough to God. I feel so grateful right now. I don't know how to describe my happiness," he smiled sitting on the bed. They got back to the hotel to collect their luggage.
"Have you both packed all your stuff?" Came in Ms. Russell.
"Yeah," Amaya responded.

Everyone left for the airport. Samuel was provided with a supporter which he had to use until his left hand cures. They headed for the airport around 2 PM.

"Kindly fasten your seatbelts," the announcement was made on the flight.

The air hostesses started giving the instructions, while Amaya helped Samuel with the seat belt. They reached the airport by 9:30 PM. They took 2 taxis and went their way. Samuel went with his mom while Daisy went with Amaya to her place. Everyone, that day was exhausted. As soon as they reached home, they slept because they had already been served with their dinners on the flight.

"So, how about getting together today at my place?"
"Today? All of a sudden? Is everything alright?" Amaya hesitated a bit.
"Yeah, actually it's my birthday today, so,"

"Oh, I'm so sorry, I did not know that. Happy Birthday, Sam! I'm so sorry for not knowing," Amaya got a bit hesitant.
"Oh no, it's fine. It's completely fine. I only did not tell you. And mom forgot due to a lot of office work. So, you need not be sorry. At all," he smiled.
"And yes, thank you for your wish," he added. Both of them smiled.
"So, when are you coming today?" he asked.
"At 6, if it's fine?"
"Perfect! I'll wait for you, he said blushing.
"Yeah," she said, blushing a little bit. Another minute of awkward silence.
"Okay then. I must go now. I've to complete some office work. So, I have to go," Amaya said in a low tone.
"Um yeah, okay then. Bye, Bye. And oh yes, thank you for your invite," she smiled.
"My pleasure,"

Both of them cut the call blushing.

"So, where do I start now? Oh God, there is so much work to do right now. Ugh!" Amaya thought, quite tense. "Anyways, I should get going and finish my office work first.

After working continuously for 6 hours, Amaya finally got up.

"I am probably going to take a nap now. I'm so exhausted,"
"Hey Girl!" Daisy entered Amaya's room while eating some ice cream.
"Hey! You must be hungry. Let me make something for you. This ice cream is not enough," Amaya said.
"Not really. I have already eaten the pizza that was left and I'm full now," Daisy smiled.
"You should have told me. I could have made something fresh for you. What was the need to eat the left out?"
"Naah, it's all fine. I did not want to disturb you," Daisy said, slurping her ice cream.
"Oh-okay. No worries. By the way, I am going to take a quick nap right now before we prepare to leave," Amaya said hurriedly.

"Prepare to leave? But where?" Daisy was confused.
"Oh God, I am so sorry, I completely forgot to tell you. Actually, it is Sam's birthday today, so he invited us to his place tonight," Amaya blushed a little.
"OMG! That is great. I am so excited now since this is not going to be another boring day," Daisy said finishing her ice cream.
"Okay so, I got to take a nap now so, bye," Amaya ran to her room.
"Um, okay. I will wake you up by 5 then," Daisy said, standing down the stairs.
"Okay!" Amaya responded.

Daisy was watching tv when she realized that it was 5.

"Amay!!" Daisy called Amaya sitting down the hall. "Hey! Wake up sleeping beauty. We need to get ready!" she continued calling her up.
"Yeah, just a minute," Amaya responded half asleep in bed.
"Not even a single minute am I going to give you. Get up lazy!" Daisy got up from the couch.
"Now I should go and choose my dress," Daisy took a stretch yawing and went to her room.
"Why does it get so lazy getting up, every time?" Amaya stood up, yawning.
Amaya and Daisy met in the living room, after getting ready.
"OMG! How do you always manage to look so damn gorgeous huh?" Daisy was startled after looking at Amaya's beauty.
"Ha ha, nice joke buddy," Amaya laughed.
"C'mon let's go now otherwise we would be late," Daisy took Amaya's hand and rushed.

AFTER REACHING SAMUEL'S PLACE

"Happy Birthday Sam!" Amaya and Daisy wished together joyously after entering his home.
"Thank you so much!" his face was beaming with happiness. He couldn't resist glaring at Amaya and her beauty.
"I'm so sorry girls, I totally forgot to tell you both about his birthday

yesterday. I was just too much involved in the office work that I forgot," Ms. Russel came to them and hugged them.
"That's completely fine mom," Amaya said.
"Oh, sweetie. What would you like to have for starters? Drinks or some Snacks?"
"Drinks, we can have first," Daisy responded.
"Yeah, we can start with having some juice," Amaya added.

Daisy helped with bringing up the glasses. Amaya brought up the juice bottles.

"Cheers!" Everyone held up their juice glasses. Amaya's phone buzzed. It was Nicole's email regarding the date, time and venue for his wedding.
"Oh My God!" Amaya kept her hand on her head.
"What happened? All good?" Daisy asked.
"I completely forgot! Nicole's wedding is to be held this month and I completely forgot about it," Amaya got tense.
"Oh, when did this happen? I had no idea, otherwise, I would have noted it somewhere," Daisy said.
"When I met him about 3 months back. He told me about him proposing to his sister's best friend and that they had to get married after four months. Due to the trip and Sam's accident, I completely forgot. We have tons of work and shopping to do now," Amaya stood up tensely.
"Calm down Amay. We are all in this together and we'll divide the tasks. Together, we'll be able to do everything in time," Samuel went beside Amaya with the help of his arm support and held her hand.
"Yeah, I hope so," Amaya said.

Both of them looked at each other and smiled. Ms. Russell went and brought the cake.

"So, birthday boy, make a wish and cut the cake," Daisy said.
"My only wish that I want God to fulfil is to give my mom the longest life that she deserves and to always keep her happy. After my dad's passing, my mom has always made sure to provide me with the best life and has been

supporting me ever since," a tear rolled down both his and Ms. Russell's eyes.

Amaya smiled and was very happy to see Samuel's kind gesture towards his mom.

"So, everyone let's get the real party started!" Ms. Russell exclaimed.
"I would like to present something in front of you all," Amaya said.
"What?" Daisy asked.
"Look for yourself," Amaya took a remote, all the lights went out and she played a short presentation through the projector.

The screen displayed Samuel's pictures, starting from his childhood ones and in the background played a poem by Amaya, which said,

"I met a man, he was tall, ahem he was a gentleman after all. It was his sweet face, which showed so much grace. A man with a huge heart, telling his good qualities, from where do I even start? His name was Samuel, always trying to act like a fool.

Showering his love and silliness everywhere,

I knew something was special about him at his first glare.

With time now, we are here,

Samuel you're so special to me, never ever change because you are rare,"

With this, the presentation ended and everyone in the room had tears in their eyes. Ms. Russell went and hugged Amaya.

"This was so pure, sweetheart," Ms. Russell said. Samuel could not stop his happy tears.
"This was," he paused.
"Can I please hug you Amaya?" he spoke again.

Amaya went to him and they both hugged. Endless emotions were reflected with this hug.

"This was so beautiful Amay," Daisy said.
"But when did you make it?" she further asked.
"During my free time," Amaya answered.

No one understood but Ms. Russell understood that Amaya loved Samuel and she also understood that Amaya was confused about her feelings and so, was not going to confess them to Samuel. But she decided to bring them both together by making them realize the truth.

"Now Amaya will propose to my son, I assure," Ms. Russell whispered to herself. After that everyone had dinner together and afterwards Amaya and Daisy headed back home.

CHAPTER FIFTEEN

It was 8 in the morning when Amaya woke up.

"Sam? Wake up," she was still sleepy as she woke up and sat on the bed. She forgot that Samuel was not there. He had gone back to his home along with his mother. As soon as she moved her hand, to wake him up, she realized that he was not there.

She wondered why she had that illusion of him being there beside her. She got up and went to make herself some coffee.

"It ain't me!" Daisy put up some music and started singing along, dancing in her comfy pyjamas.
"Good morning gorgeous!" Amaya smiled.
"Good morning love! I got some good news for you," Daisy jumped in excitement.
"Tell me about it," with a cup of coffee in her hand, Amaya listened.
"That guy whom I met at the hotel? Down the street?"
"Yeah, the one, for whom you had been shouting from the balcony, right?" Amaya sipped her coffee.
"Yes, that's the one I'm talking about right now," Daisy continued, "I found him on Facebook and guess what? He works as a manager in the company I'm going to work here for!"
"Woah! Tell me you're lying," Amaya kept her coffee aside.
"No, I'm not, ha-ha," Daisy said.
"Well, I never thought something like this would happen," Amaya laughed.

"Hello?"
"Hey," It was Samuel.

"Oh, hi. How are you doing Sam? All well?" Amaya secretly blushed without herself even knowing.
"Yes, I am doing good. How are you?"
"I am good too," there was an awkward silence for almost a minute.
"So, how about getting together today at my place?"
"Today? All of a sudden? Is everything alright?" Amaya hesitated a bit.
"Yeah, actually it's my birthday today, so,"
"Oh, I'm so sorry, I did not know that. Happy Birthday, Sam! I'm so sorry for not knowing," Amaya got a bit hesitant.
"Oh no, it's fine. It's completely fine. I only did not tell you. And mom forgot due to a lot of office work. So, you need not be sorry. At all," he smiled.
"And yes, thank you for your wish," he added.

Both of them smiled.

"So, when are you coming today?" he asked.
"At 6, if it's fine?"
"Perfect! I'll wait for you, he said blushing.
"Yeah," she said, blushing a little bit.

Another minute of awkward silence.

"Okay then. I must go now. I've to complete some office work. So, I have to go," Amaya said in a low tone.
"Um yeah, okay then. Bye, Bye. And oh yes, thank you for your invite," she smiled.
"My pleasure,"

Both of them cut the call blushing.

"So, where do I start now? Oh God, there is so much work to do right now. Ugh!" Amaya thought, quite tense. "Anyways, I should get going and finish my office work first.

CHAPTER SIXTEEN

Whatever happened last evening was proof that Amaya loved Samuel. Ms. Russell had decided to bring Amaya and her son together. No one knew what she was going to do.

The doorbell rang. Daisy went to check. It was 10:15 AM in the morning. It was a delivery guy who came to deliver a bouquet of flowers.

"Who sent these?" Daisy asked.
"I have no idea, ma'am. I was just asked to deliver these flowers," the delivery guy said.
"Um, okay," Daisy said and went inside.

Daisy's eyes caught a card kept inside the bouquet. She took out the card and it read,

"Grateful for whatever you did yesterday. I am so blessed to have you in my life,"
Yours lovingly
Sam"

"Oh, so Samuel has sent these for Amay. Such a pretty gesture of him. I'll keep these beside Amay's bed, she'll be so happy to see them when she wakes up,"

Daisy went and kept the bouquet beside Amaya's bed as a display.

Amaya woke up by 11 AM. She stretched her arms in the air and took a deep breath. That's when she saw that bouquet kept beside her bed. She wondered who sent it. She picked up the bouquet and took out the card kept in it.

She felt so happy once she finished reading that beautiful note by Samuel.

"I never expected such a beautiful gesture from Samuel. No one thanks in such a beautiful way I guess," she smiled.

Daisy came and saw Amaya sitting and blushing on the bed. She stood outside her room's door. She called out for Amaya before entering.

"Amay! You up?" Daisy said entering her room.
"Yeah. Good morning, Daisy," Amaya gave Daisy a smile.
"Good almost noon precious," Daisy giggled.
"Ha ha ha, very funny," Amaya gave her a stare.
"Would you like to have some coffee or green tea?" Daisy asked.
"Green tea will do," Amaya said, keeping the bouquet aside.
"Okay then, green tea it is," Daisy went to the kitchen.

Amaya's phone rang.

"Hello? Yes Ma'am," she said.
"Amaya, Mr. Smith called up this morning and has asked to arrange a meeting along with him and his employees for the discussion of the magazine fare coming up," Ms. Russell spoke from the other side of the phone.
"Okay, I'll finalize a date, ma'am. What date can I arrange the meeting ma'am?" Amaya asked, picking up a pen and a paper.
"Today is the 20th so, you can fix a date within the 10 days left," Ms. Russell spoke, fixing her specs, looking at the calendar.
"Okay ma'am," she said and cut the call.

Daisy came to Amaya with a cup of green tea.

"Here you go," Daisy handed over the cup to Amaya.
"Thank you!" Amaya said, sipping the green tea.

Amaya got busy in the afternoon, attending calls from her company's clients. Finally, at 8 PM the doorbell rang. It was Samuel.

"Sam! You? What are you doing here? I mean. How did you get here?" Amaya was shocked.

Samuel stood holding his support. Before any further conversation, Amaya took him in.

"My friend helped me get here," He spoke.
"Oh! Now, where is he then?" Amaya asked.
"He went back home," he scratched his head and gave a weird smile.
"Oh okay, then I'll drop you home," Amaya said, closing the door.
"No, actually," he stopped.
"Yeah say," She went to bring some water.
"I'm going to stay over here tonight," He spoke.
"Well, that's great but how come all of a sudden?" she handed the glass of water to him.
"It's been so long since I stayed here, so," He got a bit hesitant.

Daisy came downstairs.

"Hey Sam! What a pleasant surprise," She came and gave him a hug.
"Hey," he replied.

After that, they decided to watch a movie.

"Let's watch a cartoon movie!" Daisy jumped.
"Yeah, actually let's recall our childhood memories through this," Amaya smiled.
"I'll go and prepare the popcorn," Daisy ran to the kitchen.
"Let's sit on the mat today," Samuel said, getting up. Amaya helped him get up and sit down.
"Let's watch the Tom and Jerry movie," Amaya and Samuel coincidentally spoke together. Both then looked into each other's eyes and got lost. Daisy

then cleared her throat, breaking both of their eye contact.
"Oh, yes, that is one of my favourite childhood movies," Daisy said happily.

Everyone sat on the sofa together and watched the movie giggling all the time, eating popcorn.

"Childhood, according to me, is a time full of happiness and joy. We as children never cared about the sorrows in the world and just enjoyed every moment. That's the best part of childhood for me," Amaya smiled.
"Absolutely!" Daisy said.

Whereas, Samuel gave Amaya a decent smile.

CHAPTER SEVENTEEN

Both Amaya and Samuel slept hugging each other. Amaya woke up and realized that both of them hugged and slept. Amaya was very furious to know about her feelings now. She went to her room and saw a note that was kept on the table. It was Daisy's note. She had left for one of the weddings in her family at 6 AM and would be returning the next day.

"I must freshen up now and then complete finalizing the dates and timings of the meetings," Amaya went to get ready.

She came and prepared herself and Samuel some coffee.

"Hey, Sam. Wake up," Amaya kept his coffee on the table.
Samuel woke up yawning. "Hey! Good morning, Amaya,"
"Good morning, Sam. I have made you some coffee," Amaya smiled.

Samuel, after drinking the coffee, went freshening up. He came to the kitchen, wanting to prepare breakfast.

"Hey? Leave these. You are not well right now," Amaya took away the utensil from Samuel.
"Why? Can I not even prepare breakfast?" Samuel made an innocent face.
"This innocent act won't work on me," Amaya said.
"Fine," Samuel went to the garden to water the plants.
"What can I do to bring that precious smile to his face?" Amaya thought. "He has not had that precious smile since his accident. I remember how warmly he smiled before the accident,"
"Wait! I have an idea," Amaya turned on some music, went to the garden,

took the water pipe from Samuel's hands and held it high. The water drained through the pipe on both of them. It was the exact same moment that they had experienced when they first met.
"Revenge huh?" Samuel smiled.
"I guess so," Amaya threw the pipe towards the pole where it got stuck just as it happened the last time.

Amaya took Samuel's hand and danced, supporting him. Samuel finally got to smile wholeheartedly.

"That precious smile is back," Amaya murmured.
"What?" Samuel asked as Amaya could not take her eyes off him.
"Why am I doing this? What's happening to me?" Amaya thought to herself.
"Hello?" Samuel again asked.
"Nothing," Amaya smiled.

They both went and changed their outfits, after which they had their breakfast.

"By the way, where is Daisy?" Samuel asked, taking a bite of bread.
"She has gone to attend one of her family's weddings. She will be back tomorrow," Amaya sipped her green tea.
"Oh okay," he spoke.
"We too have to attend a wedding; you remember that right?" Amaya asked.
"Yes, I remember. We need to get prepared for that too," Samuel drank his green tea.
"Well, I had to tell you something," she said, being a bit hesitant.
"Yeah say?" he continued drinking his tea.
"We need to prepare a couple of dances for D-Day," Amaya felt weird. "Wait what? I do not know how to dance, hello?" Samuel stood up.
"Oh, then was it I dancing along with myself in the garden? Not once but twice. And at the cruise dinner? Amaya stared at him.
"Oh that," Samuel paused.
"No more excuses, I need," Amaya pointed at him.
"Oh okay, whatever you say," Samuel put his hands up.

"Good!" she smiled.

In the evening, they started with their practice.mAt night they both lay down on the grass, gazing at the sky.

"Have we even bought a gift to give?" Amaya asked, looking towards the sky.
"Yeah, Daisy bought it the day before, she told me," Samuel said.

They then both faced each other.

"You are beautiful," Samuel faced Amaya.
"You too Sam," Amaya smiled.

Both of them went back in and slept.

CHAPTER EIGHTEEN

A day is left for the wedding now. Amaya wanted to present herself in a very simple way. She had to shop today. Waking up around 7 AM, she went to get ready. She straight away went and sat on her desk. Opening the laptop, she started doing her office work. She had a meeting scheduled for her today. She made herself a cup of coffee before the meeting started. She had a ton of work for today, from completing the files and attending the meeting to shopping for the wedding the next day.

Samuel woke up around 10 AM, while Amaya's meeting was still going on. Looking at her responsibility, he was motivated to start working again. He went to get ready and prepared breakfast for both him and Amaya. She got free by 11 AM and after all, took a deep breath.

She was surprised after she found out that Samuel had already made breakfast. But she was worried at the same time since he was not perfectly fit yet. He was not there at that moment.

Amaya had breakfast and continued with her work again.

"Such a hectic day it is already, I don't know how I will be able to shop for tomorrow. I feel so tired," Amaya's thoughts gathered up in her head.

Samuel came back home with the grocery basket in his hand.

"Where were you?" Amaya asked, standing at the door.
"Just went to buy some groceries," Samuel kept the grocery basket on the kitchen slab.
"But you are not completely fit right now Sam! You should not exhaust

yourself for now," Amaya said.
"I know. But if I don't start from somewhere, how will I recover then?" he sat on the sofa, with the help of his support.
"I understand what you are trying to say. I just want you to not start straight from exhausting yourself. You can start by going on morning walks?" she stood on his side.
"Alright. I will start by going on walks every morning," he said.
"Good. I'll be free in a few minutes and after that, we can go shopping tomorrow shopping," she clapped her hands and rushed towards her room to continue her office work.

Samuel switched on the television and lay down on the couch. After 50 minutes Amaya got free from her work. She took a deep breath and had some water. Her phone rang. It was Daisy.

"Hey! By what time is your flight?" Amaya asked.
"My flight is at 2 PM and I'll be landing by 4 PM. I was wondering if you could pick me up from the airport?" Daisy asked.
"Yeah, sure. Call me once you land and receive your luggage. I'll be there," Amaya smiled.
"Okay then, I'll be waiting. I am texting you the rest of the details," Daisy hung up.

In a hurry, Amaya rushed downstairs and got her bag, keeping the card, a bottle and her mobile in it.

"Woah, what is this hurry for?" Samuel stood up.
"We need to go now. It's 1 PM right now and we have exactly 3 hours to shop for tomorrow and eat lunch," She wore her shoes.
"Why? Do we need to go elsewhere?" he asked.
"Yes. Daisy called just a minute back. We need to pick her up from the airport. Her flight will be landing by 4 PM," Amaya hushed.
"Oh alright. Let's go," he said, switching off the television.

Amaya drove to the shopping galleria 12 streets away. They first headed towards the clothing store.

"Excuse me? Could you please show him some outfits for a wedding?" she called the person showing the outfits in a hurry.
"Sure ma'am," the help said.
"Hey, what now? Why are you in a hurry now?" Samuel asked.
"I have to go and shop for some accessories first. I'll be back in 15 minutes," she said and before Samuel could say anything she went out of the store.

Amaya came back after 15-20 minutes and started exploring the store. She was very confused about what was to be worn at the wedding.

Then after all the searching, her eyes caught a very beautiful dress. It was a peach-coloured gown, very decent and beautiful. Just as Amaya liked a dress to be.

She went to the trial room to try the dress. The dress fit her perfectly well as if it was made for her. She looked extremely beautiful. And no one could even imagine how she would look at the wedding, the next day.

"Tomorrow is going to be a very big day," Amaya looked at the accessory bag kept on the side, the ones she bought just now.

The clothing was all selected and now was the time to shop for the footwear.

"It's 2:25 PM already!" Samuel exclaimed in a worried tone.
"I know. We need to be free by 3:50 PM otherwise we will have to postpone things and come a" he said.

At around 3:45 PM they reached the McDonald's to fetch burgers and coke for themselves. They did not have enough time to sit and eat, so they got the food packed and left by 4:00 PM.

"Oh no. I need to drive and will not be able to eat the food. I guess I would have to eat the food after reaching home," Amaya fastened her seat belt.

While she was driving, suddenly, Samuel took out a burger and insisted on making her eat with his help.

Amaya agreed and he helped her with eating the burger. He fed her the burger.

"I know that he has some feelings for me. But what are they?" Amaya thought while eating.
"This is love. I love him!" thinking this, she stared at him and smiled at him.
"That smile. That damn smile!" Samuel thought.

They reached the airport by 4:20 PM. Daisy was already waiting.

"Hey, guys! I am back!" Daisy said excitedly.
"Hey, Dora!" Amaya said, hugging her while sitting in the driver's seat.
"How was the wedding?" Samuel asked.
"It was ah-mazing!!" Daisy exclaimed.

Amaya drove back home. Meanwhile, Samuel had his burger. They reached home in half an hour.

"There's something stuck beside your mouth," Amaya said while Samuel was stepping out of the car.
"Where?" he asked and sat down again.

Amaya took out her handkerchief and gently scrubbed it beside his mouth. At one point, both of them got lost in each other's eyes for half a minute.

"Oh great! Not again," Daisy thought to herself while holding back her smile.
"A small piece of tomato, it was," Amaya told while keeping back the handkerchief.

Both smiled and got out of the car. Amaya brought in all the shopping baggage.

"Let us all rest for some time since it has been such a hectic day for us all," Amaya served the water.
"Yes. The day has been just so exhausting!" Daisy sat on the sofa.
"After all, tomorrow we need to attend the wedding ceremony which in itself is very exhausting," Samuel added.

Everyone slept for some time. At around 7:30 PM, everyone woke up. Daisy was busy listening to some music, putting her headphones on.

"I'll make myself a cup of coffee. It feels so relaxing to have a cup of coffee," Amaya prepared coffee in the kitchen.

Samuel was reading a book in his room. Amaya took her laptop and coffee and sat on the lawn.

"A cup of coffee + work + nature = perfect!" she said out loud and then started working.

After an hour everyone came to the dining area. Daisy had made pizza and pancakes for dinner. Everyone had their dinner in time and left for bed.

CHAPTER NINETEEN

The day for which everyone was excited had come.

"I am so happy for Nico!" Amaya smiled as she woke.

She went and freshened up in time. It was 7:30 AM when everyone else woke up. Whereas, Amaya made herself some coffee and got the breakfast ready for everyone. She went to the lawn and had her coffee along with reading a novel.

After a while, she put her headphones on and started dancing in her room, going with the flow of the song, "It Ain't Me" by Selena Gomez.

She got flashbacks and everything that had happened to her to date, from meeting Samuel to the accident and then the recovery.

All of a sudden, the lyrics were making perfect sense to her.
She stopped and said, "It was always love," she smiled and looked in the mirror and repeated, "It was always love," and saw glimpses at the small baggage kept along with the rest of the shopping baggage. She picked up her phone.
"I need your help," she said.

After 2 hours everyone went to get dressed up. Everyone got ready within 40-45 minutes. Amaya was just simply dolled up. She has always had a different charm on her face and today, she was carrying that charm along with her heart full of love.

"How can you be such a stunner? You always manage to look perfect," Daisy

said. Samuel was shaken after having had a glimpse at Amaya's beauty.
"How could she consistently be able to make me fall for her again and again?" Samuel thought to himself.
"How am I looking?" Amaya asked Samuel.
"I have no words. You always end up looking the most beautiful of all," he said.

Both of them blushed.

"Well, we should probably head for the marriage now. Or else we'll be late," Daisy took Amaya out with her, holding her arms.
"I am going to drive today. It's always you both driving," Daisy jumped into the driving seat.
"Fine," Amaya sat at the back along with Samuel, keeping the gifts in the front seat.

After 2 hours, they reached the wedding venue.

"Let me pick up the gifts. You go along with Samuel," Daisy got out of the car.

After the vows were taken, everyone went for the dance. It was already dark by then. The lighting in the farmhouse was just beautifully extravagant.

"Hey, Daisy, where is Amaya?" Samuel asked in a worried tone.
"She must be here only," Daisy took a glimpse around.
"I have searched for her everywhere. She is not here. Could you go check the bathroom?" he spoke.
"Yeah, let me go and search for her," Daisy rushed towards the bathroom.

Amaya could not be found there either. After 10 minutes, while returning to the hall, Daisy heard her name being called.

"Dora!" Amaya called out for her in a loud tone.

Daisy followed the voice and there she was, standing in the back lawn of the farmhouse, all decorated with lights and flowers.

"Amaya, what are you doing here? I have been searching for you everywhere," Daisy hugged Amaya.
"Could you please get Samuel here?" Amaya spoke.
"What? But why? Is everything alright?" Daisy was interrupted by Amaya.
"Yes, everything is perfect. Just bring him here," Amaya held both of her hands with glitter in her eyes.
"Okay," Daisy ran in and brought Samuel out.

It was pitch dark when they both came outside.

"The day we met; I never thought a day like this would ever happen. I am at a loss for words on how to express what I feel for you. You have always been by my side no matter what, supported me in every way and most importantly respected me all the way. I have always had some feeling in me whenever you have been around. Butterflies crowded my heart whenever I saw you. But it was so confusing for me to understand this one goddamn thing, that was hidden, deep inside my heart. And that is I love you! Yes, I love you, Sam! Truly and deeply," the lights turned on. It was Amaya who came and stood in front of him. "From all the silly moments that we have had, be it us dancing randomly on the streets, annoying each other or gazing at the stars together. Each moment I have loved you but realized it so late. I guess it is all because of fate, wanting us to be together, I guess? Maybe I have noticed that love for me in your eyes every time we glanced at each other".
Bending on her knees, she spoke, "I never asked you for a gift but now I am. Can I get the gift of being your better half? Will you marry me? Please?" Both had tears in their eyes.
"How do I even react at the moment? I have loved you since I met you. You guessed it right. But I never imagined you even giving me a bit of that love since I deemed myself unworthy of it. But here this happened. It was a complete miracle. Fate probably wanted us to realize our love for each other," saying this, Samuel threw his support down and sat on his knees. "Miss Amaya, I will be utterly blessed to have you as my better half. I love you!" he

hugged Amaya.
"I love you!" Amaya smiled with tears full of happiness.

Both exchanged rings that very moment. Amaya had already bought the rings with the help of Nico.

"Woohoo, finally!" Daisy jumped in excitement. Everyone around clapped.

"By the way, with the help of whom did you plan this proposal?" Daisy asked. Amaya pointed towards Nico. Music played in the background. Everyone danced with double joy.

CHAPTER TWENTY

After a month Samuel got rid of his support and could walk freely as before. Both Amaya's and Samuel's parents were there by then. Both of them got married on 20th December, following both the Indian and American wedding traditions separately.

It was time for Amaya to finally walk down the aisle. This time, both the bride and groom looked extremely charming due to the love they carried for each other in their hearts.

Hugging Samuel, Amaya whispered in his ear, "These were the best 365 days for me since I met you,"
"Mine too," Samuel tenderly kissed Amaya's forehead.

Joining heads, both shared smiles.

After having lived through all the sadness and the laughter, finally came their "happily ever after!"

CHAPTER TWENTY-ONE

Amaya and Samuel started fresh with their lives together, as a newlywed couple now. Ms. Russell threw a party in the office soon after the wedding. Everyone in the office congratulated the new couple.

"This is too new. A new beginning. A new chapter in life." Amaya said.
"You are going to learn a lot now, what it is like having a companion by your side until the very end. Whatever you handled alone all these years will finally get a backbone to support you in your ups and downs. I am very sure; you both will handle marriage in a lovely way." Ms. Russell hugged Amaya.
"I am grateful to have the two strongest and the most beautiful ladies in my life. Here's a toast to both my lovelies." Samuel threw a toast.

At night, after having dinner, Amaya planned to set up an arrangement to lie outside, in the garden with Samuel.

With two mugs of warm water, Samuel came and sat with her outside.

"Hello, Husband." Amaya giggled.
"Hello, wifey." Samuel kissed Amaya on the cheek.
"What's it like, being married, for you?" Amaya asked sipping from the mug.
"Well, a slight correction. What's it like, being married to the most beautiful woman?" He laughed.
"You're too good at flirting huh?" she smiled.
"A slight correction here, again. Not flirting, it's loving ma'am. I love you with all of my heart, my mind and my soul." Samuel said.
"I too love you and I promise to be your headache." Amaya giggled and hugged Samuel.

They both lay down, gazing at the stars under a cosy night sky.

"I love this and I am grateful to have you as my husband. Thank you for choosing me and loving me, just the way I am. You are my star, Sam." Amaya smiled.
"I am the most grateful here to have got you as my soulmate. You will forever be my darling baby." He pulled her cheeks.

Under the cold-warm sky, we stare at the midnight stars.

I love you with all of my heart, is all that I am left with, to say.

www.ingramcontent.com/pod-product-compliance
Lightning Source LLC
LaVergne TN
LVHW090131160826
845673LV00017B/2179
* 9 7 9 8 8 9 6 9 9 1 0 4 5 *